THE TROUBLE AT AQUITAINE

Nancy Livingston

St. Martin's Press
New York

This book has absolutely nothing to do with anyone alive or dead, nor is there a telephone box outside Pickering Police station.

Library of Congress Cataloging in Publication Data

Livingston, Nancy.
   The trouble at Aquitaine.

   I. Title.
PR6062.I915T7   1986   823′.914   85-25157
ISBN 0-312-81975-7

First published in Great Britain by Victor Gollancz Ltd.

First U.S. Edition

10 9 8 7 6 5 4 3 2 1

TO NANCY, WITH LOVE. NL

Chapter One

"AQUITAINE CASTLE WAS built as a gift for his wife by Henry the Second. On their tenth wedding anniversary he imprisoned her in it. . ." Mrs Burg paused.

Hugh was impressed. Could he, when he returned home, imprison Marion in their four-bedroomed detached or was there something forbidding it in the mortgage? His ulcer began a slow burn: umbilical proof that he and she were still one flesh.

From behind her Reception desk, Mrs Burg continued. "The castle has been the home of the Willoughby family since 1503. They once held the title of Earls of Pickering too, but in 1789, the then Earl Willoughby took his family to Paris for a holiday when the Revolution was at its height. His understanding of the situation was limited. When the natives addressed him as 'citizen', he retaliated by calling them 'bloody foreigners'. He might have avoided the guillotine even so, because the French were reluctant to behead a man whose name they couldn't pronounce, but the Earl rejected all suggestions that he contribute to the new Republic as sheer extortion. He mounted the scaffold accompanied by his Countess and all but one of their children.

"The boy who survived had not been to Eton so understood French tolerably well. He offered to marry the extremely ugly daughter of the head jailer without a dowry. He also agreed, at his father-in-law's suggestion, to repudiate the title until France was back to normal. Unfortunately he was killed at Waterloo, having founded the present line but while fighting on the wrong side.

"The present owners — who opened the castle as a health clinic in 1979 — are known therefore as Colonel and Mrs Willoughby. You will notice that their armorial bearings still include a guillotine. It is believed that the two fingers beneath represent triumph over adversity. Would you like to see your room?"

Hugh's smile was that of a man who has made the wrong choice but paid a deposit. "Is there anyone to help with my bags?"

Mrs Burg moved with difficulty. Hugh's professional eye had diagnosed an arthritic back. Now he saw her bunions. She looked round the vast entrance hall. "There is a man somewhere. . ." One mottled hand waved feebly as though trying to conjure him out of thin air. "Unfortunately he doesn't appear to be about."

Hugh stared at the leather suitcase his father had given him for his 21st. It weighed a ton even when empty. Mrs Burg's bunions appeared beside it.

"Would you like me to help with your luggage?"

"No, no!"

His smile hung rictus-like now because it had nowhere to go. He shouldered his tweed coat, overnight bag and finally the case. The climb from the car park — across a moat and over slippery cobbles — had nearly finished him. Now this. Perhaps his father had intended he should die young? Neither parent had liked Marion. Were their two ghosts manipulating his quick demise so that he could rejoin them in the next world?

He must try to rid his mind of these wild fantasies. He was here to enjoy himself, to refresh both mind and body. The locum was costing a fortune so the sooner he started, the better. Gritting his teeth, Hugh set off behind Mrs Burg.

But where was the comfort promised in the brochure? 'Well-furnished rooms, each with its own log fire. . . Colonel and Mrs Willoughby will restore each of their guests to their full potential as human beings. . .' This great stone corridor hadn't been mentioned. Cold air blew in gusts along the length of it, lifting coir matting and making the suits of armour rattle.

Mrs Burg shivered. "We're getting rid of the smell."

"Smell!" A vision danced in front of Hugh's eyes of long-dead

6

Willoughbys, mouldering beneath the flagstones, fingers still rampant.

"Of hot food. Guests are allowed one hot meal on their final night. The smell can be disturbing for those remaining with us, especially anyone on — the liquid diet."

She managed to invest this phrase with a significance all its own. "D'you think I shall have to have that? The liquid diet?" Her glance appeared to Hugh to assess not only his chances of salad but of life itself.

"Oh, yes — liquids. I shouldn't think there's any doubt about that."

Suddenly he realized he wasn't merely overweight, he was obese; flabby with adipose deposits furring up his arteries in a moving blanket of slurry. He tautened his stomach muscles. His ulcer tweaked reproachfully. "Hang on a minute. Got a pain." Mrs Burg waited patiently. It happened every week. They came, expecting miracles. So foolish. She remembered this was Hugh's first visit and pushed open an imposing oak door.

"This is the library. Guests are requested not to smoke in here." Hugh recognized page two of the brochure and inhaled warmth gratefully.

"Oliver Cromwell used this room during one of his northern campaigns."

"Did he really?"

Had the iron fist actually rested on that massive table now littered with copies of *The Field* and leaflets from the Ministry of Agriculture?

"He sat there when he signed the death warrant for three thousand Irish soldiers."

Hugh tried to fight back. He had come here at considerable expense. "What a wonderful view of the park. No doubt he appreciated that?"

"Victims of the Black Death are buried beneath those trees. There was a lot of it about in the fifteenth century."

He craved the sanctuary of his room but Mrs Burg closed the door of number eight before he could glimpse inside.

7

"Not quite ready I'm afraid. The previous occupant — one of our regulars — had an unfortunate accident in there last night." She sighed. "So sad. He's becoming quite senile in many little ways."

Hugh felt savage. If he'd had any strength left he would have wrenched the nearest pike from the wall and cleft Mrs Burg's skull in half. She turned and smiled at him. Bushy eyebrows met in a solid line of bristle above her thin nose.

"Why not leave your things here? It must be nearly time for tea." As if in answer, a distant bell rang.

"Where do they serve that?"

"In the Solarium." Her gnarled finger pointed back along the way they'd come. Hugh went, trying to slough off thoughts of murder.

He was surprised he hadn't noticed the padded door before. It was opposite the one to the library and set into the thickness of the wall. There were no windows on this side of the corridor, only the one aperture in the whole expanse of stone.

As he'd driven up, Hugh had noticed that the castle was odd, being three-sided, not rectangular. The south-west wall had disappeared entirely. In its place was a high glass dome. He wondered what had happened but the explanation was simple. In 1979, when the Colonel had come into his inheritance, his wife declared she had no intention of enduring medieval discomfort. Instead, she would turn their fortress into a temple worthy of Sybaris. She lured the south Yorkshire representative of the society for the Preservation of Rural Castles up on a visit and persuaded him that the Victorian buttresses outside the south-west wall were an anachronism. So they were, but they were also its only means of support. The unfortunate demolition crew hadn't even time to reverse their bulldozers before twelfth-century granite engulfed them.

Mrs Willoughby, though sympathetic, was triumphant. Her courtyard was now open to the sunlight without even a murmur from the National Trust. She comforted the south Yorkshire representative, sent him quickly on his way and began her alterations. A swimming pool was excavated, half-covered by

8

the huge glass dome. Beneath this she created a tropical paradise. Guests could plunge into warm scented water, surrounded by lush greenery, swim outside to where the pool continued as part of the terrace and take a cursory look at the moors before diving back under the wall of the dome into the heady tropical womb. This then, was the Solarium.

Mrs Willoughby ordered a blue plaque to commemorate the demolition crew. The President of the Society for the Preservation of Rural Castles unveiled it. High on the wall, beneath frangipani and profuse bougainvillaea, it slowly rusted.

Hugh read in neat gold letters — 'Solarium: please close the door'. He pushed. It opened the other way. Surprised, he pulled and instantly felt a wave of humidity wash over him, leaving his shirt stuck to his body. There was a cacophony of sound — voices topping the wild unearthly cries of peacocks. A lack of oxygen made him gasp. One voice rose above the rest, high-pitched, accented with a curious nasal giggle, "I spy strangers. That is what you say in England, yes? When there is a foreign body?"

Five people stared at Hugh: he was the only one in a suit. Too late, he remembered the brochure — 'casual clothes at all times' — he'd been caught out by that one before. Now it looked as if he'd been caught by it again. Everyone else appeared to be wearing towelling robes. He recalled the elderly M & S dressing gown, packed in the confident assumption no human eye would see it. Could he possibly wear that in here? He took a deep breath, determined to bluff it out, to give the impression he was so high-powered, so steeped in business that he hadn't had time to pack properly, but his glasses steamed up. He tripped, falling headlong down a flight of stone steps and into their midst.

There were noises of concern and the ineffectual laying on of hands. Above it all a woman's silvery bell-tone insisted, "We only say that in parliament, Mr Von Tenke, never at Aquitaine. Besides I feel sure this isn't a stranger but one of our new guests. Mr Godfrey, isn't it?" She went on uncertainly, for Hugh had arrived at her feet and could no longer be ignored.

"I hope you haven't broken anything, Mr Godfrey?"

9

Foolishly, Hugh shook his head. Flashes of lightning came and went behind his eyes.

"Welcome, welcome to Aquitaine."

Half-blind, he looked up at her beige figure. "Might I have a cup of tea? With milk and sugar — Aaah!" One of the helping hands had touched the small of his back, now red hot and hurting from the fall. His ulcer sent a spurt of pure bile into his throat. "Plenty of milk, please," he gasped but the beige one reproved him, "Oh, I'm afraid not, Mr Godfrey. Camomile sweetened with honey, perhaps. We must start as we mean to go on, mustn't we?" Around her, other penitents nodded. If they were suffering, so by God must he. Virginia Fawcett, secretary and personal assistant to Mrs Willoughby, turned to the circle and announced, "This is Mr Godfrey, ladies and gentlemen. On his first visit." Hugh's elbow throbbed but she grasped it firmly, thus preventing him wiping his glasses.

"May I introduce Mrs Arburthnot. She's been here so many times, haven't you Sheila?" Hugh saw something blurred and herbaceous, topped by pinkness. Out of it came such refinement, he had to steel himself not to shrink away.

"Thirteen times, or is it more? I never can remember! On this occasion, I'm in number three, thanks to dear Virginia." Hugh felt the scratch of a lace hanky as Mrs Arburthnot clasped his hand in her own soft one. "Number three is the Plantagenet suite," she told him, her voice lowered to the level of intimacy. "It has its own private amenities. I never like to be without those, do you?"

Hugh didn't. "What about number eight?" he asked. "Has that got them?" Behind him, a peacock screamed derisively. The hairs on Hugh's neck prickled but he tried to keep the chit-chat flowing, "The bloke there last night had a bit of a problem apparently." His shins were hurting now. He desperately wanted to rub them but Miss Fawcett seized his arm again.

"It wasn't that kind of accident," she hissed, "and number eight has half-facilities, which means a bidet." Her voice resumed its former sweetness. "This is Miss Brown, another guest well known to us."

This time the hand was scaly. Hugh wanted to rub his own on his trouser leg.

"D'you play croquet, Mr Godfrey?"

"I'm afraid not, no."

"Why not try and learn? We're here for a week."

The force of her argument landed as spittle on his cheek. He tried to back away but a blur moved in front of him, tall enough this time to cast a shadow across his face. Once again he heard the high-pitched nasal giggle. Miss Fawcett spoke deferentially, "This is Mr Von Tenke. He too is on his first visit — and is a friend of the family."

Her tone expressed more than words ever could. Half-blind, Hugh recognized a social divide. He himself was obviously below the salt but facing one who was above. This time, the crushing grip was as unexpected as it was painful. He cried out, missing Miss Fawcett's next words, "Ah, here's Jessie with your tea." Hugh wrenched away his hand, shaking it instinctively. He caught the edge of the saucer a smart blow and the delicate cup soared upwards. A parabola of scalding golden liquid descended, turning beige silk a dark muddy brown. It was Miss Fawcett's turn to shriek. She reached such a pitch of intensity and passion, an elderly peacock mistook it for a mating call and unfurled his tail feathers in delicious anticipation.

On a moorland plateau above Danby, a Lancia Beta crawled along a single-track road. Inside, the two women passengers were so weary they were almost beyond words. Eventually one of them spoke. "We've overshot the place by at least twenty miles."

"What absolute nonsense!"

The driver needed to be over-confident in his professional life and saw no reason to behave differently now. Jonathan P. Powers was a television producer or, as he was fond of describing it, "I'm a creative person, striving, evolving but above all structuring meaningful programmes."

Unfortunately, he'd lost the knack. Nowadays their meaning

was so banal, their structure so old-fashioned that Jonathan's position in the industry was that of a shooting star: he was on the way out. This fact struggled into his consciousness during dark night hours, making him even more aggressive. In the studios, he clung to people, forced his way into conversations which shrivelled at his approach, trying to read in other men's eyes — admiration, envy — anything but pity.

He was unwanted on this occasion but refused to admit it. Both his passengers had thought of nothing else for the past five hours. In the back, his mother was indignant. How like Jonty to ruin things. She and Clarissa had been looking forward to their holiday until he insisted on coming. She shifted in the uncomfortable seat, her hip still sore from the operation. If she and Clarissa had been in her little car, Mrs Rees would have been in the front, enjoying herself. And they would have been at their destination by now.

"Why don't you listen to her, Jonty? This is the third time we've been lost — "

"Mother, be quiet!"

Gears crashed noisily. He had forgotten these days there were five. Mrs Rees was disgruntled. It was so typical — and so unfair.

The Hon. Clarissa Pritchett closed her eyes and tried to remember why she'd ever begun an affair with Jonathan. True, ten years ago everything had been different. He'd been 'up and coming', his programmes always previewed in the Sundays, constantly nominated for BAFTA awards and she, his favourite researcher. Now they were lucky if he got a mention in the *Daily Mail*; usually it was better if he didn't. From peak time to afternoon slot in ten short years. As for their personal relationship, the future stretched in front of her as barren as the moor. If they'd been married, at least she could have demanded a divorce. Suddenly the car swerved and jerked to a stop. Eyes still closed she braced herself instinctively for the crash. Perhaps this was the answer to all her problems? Opening her eyes she found two sheep staring in at them, chewing busily.

"Bloody farmers! Those animals came straight at me!"

Jonathan jammed his thumb on the horn.

"We're on an unfenced road, that's why. We passed the warning sign way back — "

"I saw it, too. I saw that sign!" Mrs Rees was beginning to feel light-headed.

"All right, all right. Hand over the map."

He studied it casually before turning it round, his ethnic necklace tangling with the ribbon marker. Sunglasses fell from their resting place in his hair on to the bridge of his nose.

"Blast! Where d'you say we are?"

Clarissa pointed.

"But that's far too far north! Why on earth bring us all the way up here?"

She closed her eyes, this time because she didn't want to see his face, and again tried to remember what it was that had first attracted her. Her mind remained a blank.

"Clarissa, I asked you a question."

"What do you want me to do?"

"Navigate us back to Aquitaine, of course. Unless you plan spending the night up here?"

"Reverse back to the last crossroad and turn round."

"Whatever for? It's over half a mile."

"The next one's three miles further on."

"Sod that! It's wide enough to turn round here."

Opening the window, the Friend of the Earth cried, "Move you stupid animals, move!" If only these two had been available when he'd made that documentary about Abattoirs for the COI — he'd have wiped that silly grin off their faces!

The two sheep stood watching the twelve-point turn. Not since the beaching on Ararat had there been such frantic manoeuvrings. News spread by that strange alchemy Nature has instilled in all her creatures so that when it was over and Jonathan finally looked out through the windscreen back whence they'd come, he found he was facing the rest of the flock. His reaction was so predictable, Clarissa sank back in a stupor.

Mrs Rees watched as Jonathan charged about, arms flailing, screaming against the wind, forcing the sheep into a compact mass round the car, twenty deep. She tapped Clarissa on the shoulder. "Thank God you're not married to him, dear."

The unidentified helicopter swooped so uncertainly in and out of the Fylingdales Special Rules Zone, it appeared like a flight of migratory swallows on their radar screens. Inside, soft Irish voices called to one another.

"D'you know where the hell we are?"

"Over Yorkshire, I think. I'm pretty sure. I mean, if it was Lancashire, one of us would've spotted the Pennines. . . wouldn't we? Maeve, can you see a Roman road down there?"

Sean believed in a visual approach; instruments had been known to be faulty. Maeve peered. "I can't see anything because it's getting dark."

"Wouldn't you just know it. It'll be daylight still over Killemorragh but over here, it's got to get dark suddenly."

Maeve held her peace. It was well known that navigation wasn't Sean's strong point; he was better with guns. It was simply when the Americans decided one of the cell should be trained as a pilot, Sean was the obvious choice. Liam's eyesight was none too good, Kevin couldn't stay off the drink and the men in Boston emphatically did not want a female patriot flying their machine. Maeve sometimes wondered what female patriots were supposed to do anyway. She didn't like admitting it, but she was bored. The Americans didn't seem to mind the waiting. They would come over on clandestine visits, sit hours on end in the smoky pub, listening to laments for dead heroes and emerge, satisfied, starry eyed, ready to press more money into Liam's hand for the great work.

It was that money that was benefiting her now so she mustn't grumble. When they'd seen her rash, the others decided she was suffering from strain and must go to England straight away to get fit. So here she was.

She took a discreet look at the AA book strapped to Sean's thigh. He'd marked their destination with a large black cross that obliterated many salient features. It was also on the join of the page.

"Keep a look-out, will you Maeve. If this is Yorkshire, it's where the Brits do their low-level flying. Oh, d'you see that! Isn't that it?" Sean lost 500 feet and she clung to her harness but what he'd spotted failed to satisfy him. He pressed his hands over his eyes, the better to work out their position.

"Now we know the coast is behind us because both of us noticed it, and we passed a town which might or might not have been Scarborough. South is back there in England, so. . ." The helicopter began to yaw: Maeve applied a touch more left rudder. They were going round in circles but Sean hadn't noticed. "I'm thinking it can't be far from here."

"You said we could land right beside it. A Norman Castle with its own airstrip, you said."

"Well, it might or might not have a strip. The page with the symbols on has gone from me book. It might be a better idea entirely if we found a nice big field, quick. One with no power lines across it."

It was almost night. In the AA book the hills round about were coloured deepest brown.

"Okay Sean, whatever you say. But find a field that's near the place, will you."

"That's my girl."

He began an approach over Wade's Causeway.

In Reception, Jonathan had discovered the booking arrangements.

"Separate rooms? Are you mad, Clarissa!"

"I'd prefer a room of my own."

"What on earth for? I know we're here for our health — " he flashed his elderly boyish smile at the receptionist, "but surely that's carrying things too far?"

Mrs Burg looked on impassively. On the liquid diet she knew it didn't matter. She pushed three keys across the counter.

"The ladies are in rooms one and two on the ground floor. Mr Power — "

"Power*z*," said Jonathan sharply.

"You are in number five on the floor above." She looked

15

Jonathan firmly in the eye. "No doubt you can manage the luggage? There is a man but he doesn't appear to be about."

Hugh waited impatiently, obeying instructions on the card. 'All new arrivals will be seen by Dr Willoughby. Your appointment is for 6.45 sharp.' It was now 7.00 p.m. and dinner, equally sharply, at 7.30. Hugh was becoming anxious. He tried to concentrate on an edition of *Punch*, so old he thought he remembered it from his father's waiting room. The elderly woman sitting opposite leaned forward and tapped his ankle with her stick. She managed to hit the exact spot injured by his fall.

"I think your wife washed your dressing gown at the wrong temperature."

"I believe she did, yes."

"They go that colour if the water's too hot."

"Really?"

"Why not give it to Oxfam. They'll find a use for it."

There was a burst of laughter from inside the Consulting Room. Mrs Rees looked at the door with distaste. "That's my son in there. No doubt you recognized him."

"I believe I did, yes. . ."

It hadn't been easy. Jonathan featured his own profile at the beginning and end of each of his programmes but this no longer matched reality. Folds of skin softened the once taut jaw, insufficient hair revealed the flatness of the skull.

"The *Daily Telegraph* said Jonty lacked talent. . ."

Hugh warmed towards the critic but he could not think of a suitable reply. He busied himself, clearing his throat.

"He's my son by my first husband, Harold P. Powers."

"I see. . ."

"My second husband, George — he's dead too, by the way — we had no children." There was another burst of laughter from inside. Hugh resigned himself to the tête-à-tête.

"Harold was much older than I was. . . Not a nice man at all. D'you know, it never occurred to me when Jonty was a little baby that he might take after Harold. . . ?"

Hugh could think of no safe reply to this either.

"And George turned out to be perfectly horrid. I think it's unfair, to have married *two* dreadful people, don't you?"

Was there to be no escape? "It must be, yes. . ."

"Fortunately they both left me money. That's what Jonty's after of course, because the *Telegraph* was right — he has no talent — and he lives beyond his means, but I'm going to spend it. Every single blessed penny if I can." She was sitting bolt upright now, eyes shining. Hugh wondered uneasily if her tablets were in her bag: she was a 'heart' if ever he saw one. He prayed for deliverance before she got too excited. "Clarissa's going to take me gambling — "

"Mr Godfrey?"

"Doctor."

Surprised God had acted so quickly, Hugh replied automatically, but he no longer cared. Here at least was escape. He hobbled past Jonathan into the Consulting Room.

Dr Willoughby was so unlike his elder brother that following his birth, his mother was subjected to opprobrium which lasted the rest of her life. The doctor was dapper, silver-haired, with a record for productivity unrivalled throughout Harley Street. When his sister-in-law first suggested opening up the Castle to the Nouveau Gros, he recognized a splendid idea and overruled the Colonel's objections. He even approved the Solarium. Anything was better than having to do a Longleat. His brother and Consuela had no children so one day the doctor would inherit a very profitable business. He took flying lessons, his accountant offset the cost of the airstrip against tax. Dr Willoughby pointed out to the Colonel how sensible it would be to check all guests on arrival, that way any incipient coronaries might be spotted. As a result, Aquitaine's reputation among Health Farms was unblemished. No one had, as yet, died on the premises. All that was to change.

The doctor loathed night flying and was due in London in the morning. Noticing the time, he recognized his danger. He had allowed Jonathan to overrun because of the hint that a medical expert was still being sought for a series. Dr Willoughby saw

17

words filling the screen even as Jonathan spoke:

Medical Consultant to the Producer —
DR T.W.R. WILLOUGHBY

In his naïvety he never imagined that Jonathan visualized:

The doctor who advised
JONATHAN P. POWERS
wishes to remain anonymous
for professional reasons

Now Dr Willoughby moved swiftly. He hung his jacket on a chair so that the Jermyn Street label could clearly be seen and adjusted his Turnbull & Asser tie, still good in parts.

"Travelling incognito, Dr Godfrey?"

"I prefer to, on holiday. In front of other guests."

"Quite, quite. My wife insists on the same thing when we're cruising, except on Cunard, of course. I'm on their Board. Are you in general practice?"

"In Pinner."

"Ah. . ."

Which disposed of that, too.

"Would you like to take off your — garment — and stand on the scales?"

All Hugh's jockey pants sagged so he'd put on boxer shorts for this appointment. They'd been bought, he remembered, as part of his trousseau. Like his marriage they too declared themselves a failure and clung dejectedly to his hips.

The doctor's tongue clicked feverishly as he slid the weights further and further along. "Dear me, dear me, about a stone in excess, wouldn't you say?"

Hugh refused to be drawn. Catching sight of the bruising on his shins, Dr Willoughby was momentarily distracted.

"Good Heavens, how did that happen?"

"I fell down the stairs to the Solarium."

"What an extraordinary thing to do."

"If I could have a little Arnica. . . ?"

Dr Willoughby smiled at such a suggestion, darted to his

medicine cabinet and pressed a pad soaked in iodine firmly against Hugh's purple flesh. The liquid trickled over his skin, penetrating every nook and cranny, burning its way through to his tibia. He hopped round the room, sucking his breath through clenched teeth, his shorts falling to his knees. Dr Willoughby called out fretfully, "You have to give it time to work, you know. Could you lie on the couch for me?"

Like the rest of the furniture, this was a solid antique, covered in rich buttoned leather. A paper towel was placed dead centre and Hugh lowered himself on to this carefully. The doctor tapped his ankle; the reflex startled both of them. "Some nervous tension there, I fear."

"It was a blood blister. Have you got any Kleenex?"

Dr Willoughby stood well back while Hugh mopped at the stain.

"Any other — medical problems?"

"I've got an ulcer."

"Dear me, dear me." Ulcers were down-market, much better dealt with by the Health Service. Dr Willoughby's favourite patients suffered nothing more tangible than stress.

"The pressures of Pinner, no doubt?"

Suddenly, Hugh felt a need for sympathy and understanding.

"It's my wife. She's taken to sleeping with the professional at the golf club." He laughed shame-facedly. "It's affecting my acidity, I'm afraid." Dr Willoughby was made of sterner stuff.

"A golfer, eh?" he said heartily. "And what's her handicap?"

Back in the waiting room, Hugh glanced at his watch. Four minutes twenty-five seconds for £15.50 plus VAT. He needn't have worried. He'd even got time to change before dinner.

In the Edwardian wing in front of their individual log fires, other guests were dressing. On their TVs a passionate appeal for starving children in Ethiopia was in progress but they scarcely noticed. They were here to flatten their own bellies, not worry about empty swollen ones.

Sheila Arburthnot lay in her Plantagenet bath thinking

about Eric. She didn't often do this because it made her angry, which was bad for the pores. Overhead an unlikely Elinor disported herself on the ceiling, waiting for Henry to return. Sheila knew Eric was unlikely to do this. She'd seen him safely despatched at the crematorium. Nevertheless his spirit had been conjured up, meeting Valter Von Tenke again. After all these years memories flooded back, most of them irritating. Eric's last sin, the gravest of all, was one of omission. He had never told his wife that suicide invalidated insurance policies. When the solicitor had explained, shown her the clause, she still couldn't bring herself to believe it. Not that she'd said a word. She'd had enough trouble convincing the police that Eric could have tied that particular knot. Penury forced her to do a moonlight flit from the little bungalow in Changi. 'Home' was now a bed-sit behind Baker Street.

Mrs Arburthnot looked round now at the marble bathroom with its gold fittings and soft pink towels. This was the setting she deserved. She scrimped to be able to come twice a year and had convinced herself that Mrs Willoughby regarded her differently, as 'one of them'. All this could disappear because of Valter Von Tenke. To be persona non grata at Aquitaine was too terrible to contemplate, but Mrs Arburthnot forced herself to do so. Her face grew darker, the water colder, and the Badedas failed to live up to its promise.

Miss Brown's unpacking didn't take long. She tipped her suitcase on to the bed, retrieved the photograph and put it on the mantelpiece. Where she could see it. She always carried it with her. Irrefutable proof, beneath those wreaths and green turves, that Daddy was safely laid to rest.

He hadn't wanted to die. In fact, he'd made an awful fuss. The two retired schoolteachers in the flat below had been worried. They'd spoken to the doctor. He'd warned, "Keep your strength up, Miss Brown, keep your strength up or you'll never manage." But she had.

She bounced on the familiar bed — it was jolly decent of Miss Fawcett to put her in number four again — then she remembered Mr Von Tenke. Oh, bother. Fancy him turning up here. Would there be any unpleasantness? She hoped not. Absent-mindedly, Miss Brown got off the bed and flung a few garments on hangers. Never mind, she'd kept her strength up. She could cope. She'd say a little prayer, that always helped. And in an optimistic frame of mind she set off for the library.

Mrs Rees walked from her bed to the wardrobe and back again without using her stick. She was excited: rehabilitation had begun. She approved the furniture here. Solid, good quality that wouldn't give way if she leaned on it. Like the pieces she'd kept from her childhood home. She'd hang on to those when she sold the Manor. Everything else could go. She wanted nothing that reminded her of Harold. Or George. Just a little flat somewhere as a base. Brochures were spread over the dressing table, Nevada. . . Macao! She'd always wanted to go East. Clarissa would come with her — such a nice girl, far too good for Jonathan. They would have to get rid of him. At the hospital, Mrs Rees had been told she was good for another five years. She could pack quite a lot into those five years if she didn't waste any more time. Yes, they would have to shake Jonathan off. Somehow.

He himself was annoyed. No one had recognized him, or if they had, hadn't said so. Even Dr Willoughby persisted in calling him "Dimbleby". Yorkshire! Why on earth had he agreed to come here? A week is sufficiently long in any television producer's life to wipe the memory clean: Jonathan had no recollection at all of his passionate insistence. He recalled making some vague remark to Clarissa about the air up here being healthy so flung open the window and inhaled a chestful of the stuff. Instantly his body temperature dropped several degrees. He could feel it scouring his windpipe and, as it reached his lungs, form ice. My God, he might not survive this trip!

It didn't matter what Clarissa might say, she could go on her knees and beg, he was going home. Back to the warm pollution of Shepherd's Bush.

"Don't jump!"

The order exploded in Jonathan's ear. He jerked forward, losing his hold on the frame and found himself dangling half-in, half-out of the window, 50 feet above the black water of the moat.

"Help!" he yelled.

"Do not let go," Valter Von Tenke advised from the window next to his.

"Don't be bloody stupid," cried Jonathan, "there's nothing for me to hold on to — help — somebody! Get me back inside!"

The window below opened and Clarissa asked cautiously, "Jonathan? Is that you making all that racket?"

"He is leaning out of the window," Valter called, adding unnecessarily, "He could fall if he is not careful."

Clarissa looked up. Jonathan's face, puce-coloured, hung in space several feet above her own. His arms cleaved the air like a swimmer doing reverse crawl.

"Jonathan, that's very silly. And dangerous. You could split your head open diving from that height. Anyway, you can't swim," she remembered, "and the water down there is filthy."

"Get me back inside! Please!!"

"I agree with the young lady. It would be most dangerous, even for an expert. I myself would not like to — "

"GET ME BACK INSIDE!"

The other two paused. There was no doubt the request was genuine.

"You mean — you can't manage it?" Clarissa asked doubtfully.

"No, you stupid — Ahh! I'm falling!"

His body slithered a few inches nearer eternity and, as Clarissa watched, his mouth and eyes formed completely round 'O's in his face. He made a noise, a rising crescendo of pain.

"Thing — sticking in my whassit!"

From his position, Valter Von Tenke studied the situation carefully.

"It is the little piece of metal for the window handle. It pokes always upward to penetrate the little holes," he announced, demonstrating with his finger, "It is that perhaps to which he is referring?"

Clarissa asked urgently, "Can we get into your room or have you locked the door?"

"Yes — no — I can't remember!"

"I will find out for you." Valter disappeared. Further along another casement opened and a voice enquired, "Anything the matter?" Hugh was looking out of number eight.

"Good evening," Clarissa said politely, "I'm afraid Jonathan can't get back inside."

"Good Lord! That looks dangerous."

"You. . . stupid. . . pillock!" Jonathan's voice was fainter now. Clarissa heard the distant rattle of a handle. "Sounds as if you have locked the door."

"I'm going to die up here. . . Where nobody even knows me. . ."

"Oh, don't be so wet!"

They were undoubtedly acquainted, Hugh decided, but past the first fine careless rapture. He liked the look of the girl. The foreigner popped out again like Mr Punch, waving a key. "All is not lost. I am trying my own in the hole."

"Get bloody on with it then!"

"I'll give you a hand."

Hugh emerged to find Jonathan's door already open. He hurried inside. "We say three?" Valter asked. He was gripping Jonathan's trouser band. Hugh grabbed a leg. "Three," he agreed, and heaved. Valter's strength astonished him. Jonathan's body ricocheted across the room. Hugh landed on his bottom. The girl stood in the doorway, looking at them. "Hurry up, Jonathan. It's gone seven-thirty."

He crawled across to the bathroom, clutching his parts.

"How can you even mention food! Where's the Savlon?"

"You'd better go," she said to Valter and Hugh, "I can manage here. And thank you for all your help."

"Help!!" Jonathan was outraged. He knelt upright, pointing a shaking finger at Valter, "He's just tried to murder me."

*

23

A mile away, Maeve paused. She could see it clearly now, a solid mass brooding against the skyline. She couldn't fathom why part of it was missing, as if a great stone tooth had been extracted, and in the wound, red-gold phosphorescence from the Solarium suppurated. Then the moon came from behind a cloud, cauterizing everything with silver. The castle became a floodlit stage, surrounded by black hills. Maeve changed her rucksack to the other shoulder and strode out towards it.

In the Willoughbys' private apartment, Miss Fawcett wrung her hands. "I cannot think what has happened but dare we delay any longer? Jessie has already served more punch than is wise."

"You're sure Miss Kelly was making her own way here?" Consuela Willoughby asked, "and that we weren't supposed to meet her at the station?"

Miss Fawcett was hurt. Reliability was her watchword. She found Maeve's letter from among others on her clipboard and handed it over. "If she has changed her mind and come by train, Mrs Willoughby, the last one arrived over an hour ago which is why I'm so worried."

The Colonel paused in removing burrs from a wolfhound's ears. "Come, come Fawcett, she'd hardly route herself on a train, coming from Killemorragh, now would she?"

To Miss Fawcett, Ireland north or south was as uncharted as Venus. "I suppose not, no. . ."

Dr Willoughby looked out of the window at his Partenavia Victor parked beside the grass strip and resented being held up. Didn't this guest realize time was money? His money. With cloud at less than a thousand feet he wouldn't have taken off anyway but he ignored this. It was nicer to blame an Irish woman. It made him feel a better pilot.

"I had a nine o'clock appointment tomorrow. In town. Better phone my secretary and ask her to cancel, I suppose." Consuela made a sympathetic gesture. "Perhaps your patient could come back later?"

Dr Willoughby doubted it. From past experience he knew the African Minister of Supply to be both infertile and impatient. He would simply go and look for another witchdoctor. There were plenty about in Harley Street.

"All the same, I hope our missing guest isn't coming across the moor." Consuela joined her brother-in-law at the window, "D'you think we should call the hounds back in?"

The Colonel snorted. "Who on earth walks out there at this time of night? Only bloody hitch-hikers and they deserve to be eaten. Come on. We'll get a phone call later saying she's been held up. Time to press the flesh. You joining us, Tom?"

Dr Willoughby shook his head. "Certainly not," he replied emphatically, "I've been pleasant to all of them already."

Hugh felt light-headed. Was there some narcotic nestling amid the chopped mint? In the library, the happy hour seemed endless. Everyone was so cheerful, even Jonathan P. Powers. The unpleasantness upstairs was obviously forgotten. He and the foreigner were joking together — loudly — in the middle of the room. Perhaps it was the nature of Jonathan's work, flickering, insubstantial imagery that enabled him to accuse a man of murder one minute and chatter gaily to him the next. He'd certainly been rude enough in the bedroom but Von Tenke had shrugged it off. Hugh drank more punch. From nowhere it seemed, his glass was refilled. Perhaps it wasn't punch but an anaesthetic? He found he no longer cared about his stomach rumbling because he couldn't feel any pain.

He'd accounted for all those he'd met in the Solarium. With his glasses on he could see that the refined herbaceous one was a faded English rose. The hair was dry blond, the skin blotchy and Mrs Arburthnot had told him, skittishly, that she was a widow. Hugh kept well away from her.

Miss Brown had told him she was ready for anything and how about a run before breakfast? Hugh declined — 'on medical advice' — and she'd stared at him seriously, round eyes in a chubby face. "Probably just as well, Mr Godfrey. You're looking awfully seedy." Hugh was annoyed. He would get fit. He'd leave this place as fit as the next man.

The girl was with the woman he'd met in the waiting room. Now that he could see Clarissa properly, Hugh liked the look of her even more. Which was why he was keeping his distance. Lovely bones. Fine papery skin. How old was she? Thirtyish? Forget it. He'd got enough complications in his life. This was no occasion to add to them. Just concentrate on diet and exercise. All the same, what on earth did she see in that TV monkey?

There was another burst of extravagant laughter. All eyes were on Jonathan. He gestured to Clarissa, "Darling, remind me to tell you the one about the horny-eyed snail — after Mama has gone to bed, ha-ha! I say Valter," he turned his back on both women again, "that was terribly funny." Mrs Rees stared impassively. Hugh saw her lips move. "Untalented. . . totally without merit. . ." She was repeating the *Daily Telegraph's* words like a Mantra. Valter stared over Jonathan's shoulder at Clarissa. Seeing this, Hugh felt jealous, then he saw the girl notice the stare, and shiver. He wondered why.

Hugh couldn't decide about Valter at all. His height put him above everyone else, his nervous tic of a giggle and glistening lower lip made Hugh feel sweaty. Why? Was it the unexpected strength behind a feline exterior? Perhaps the bloke was an athlete? He had the dense white skin of a near albino but it was a healthy whiteness. Hugh was fed up. Here he was looking and feeling seedy, even the revolting Jonathan had a pallor, so what was this virile specimen doing at a health farm? Then he remembered. Valter Von Tenke was a friend of the Willoughbys.

The door swung open interrupting his reverie. Miss Fawcett and Mrs Burg in genteel evening black stood on either side like sentinels. "Ladies and gentlemen," Miss Fawcett announced, "may I introduce you to your host and hostess at Aquitaine, Colonel and Mrs Willoughby." Hugh wondered feebly if they were supposed to clap.

A wolfhound stalked in and flopped into a *Tatler* pose in front of the fire. The Colonel and Consuela followed, her hand resting lightly on his arm. It was a superb entrance but when

Hugh thought about it afterwards, all rather silly. The Willoughbys paused, framed in heavy oak. "Welcome, welcome everyone to our home," cried Consuela.

Sheila Arburthnot was ready. She had been here so many times — was it thirteen — and always this ritual was the same. But Jonathan was before her. With one bound he was bending over Consuela's hand. "Dear, dear Mrs Willoughby, thank you for allowing us to visit with you." He kissed her fingertips delicately. Anyone would think they weren't paying, Hugh thought indignantly.

Consuela's beauty was impressive but her breasts were amazing. Hugh appreciated fine workmanship and wondered if these were American. They pushed upwards against their silky covering and he couldn't ever remember such symmetry. She was nearly as tall as her husband but much younger, with dark gold-flecked eyes. Her skin had an infra-red glow and the raven hair would reach below her waist, Hugh decided. As she walked towards him he tried to keep his eyes on her face but it was no use. Panels of her skirt floated upwards revealing perfect legs. If she could read his thoughts, he'd be struck off. She smiled. "I gather we have to nurse you back to health, Dr Godfrey. I look forward to playing my part."

Hugh instantly thought of several ways, each exquisitely pleasurable. Mrs Willoughby banished them all in a sentence. "My exercise classes are at ten and four daily. I look forward to seeing you then." She was gone, moving to where Miss Brown stood, blushing like a schoolgirl. Did Miss Brown use a scrubbing brush on her shiny red skin, Hugh wondered. There was a mark on the seat of her skirt. Not someone who bothered with mirrors. Then he realized he himself was being watched. Powers' girlfriend — every cynical thought writ large across her face. Blast! She came across. "Quite an entrance, wasn't it. We haven't been properly introduced. I'm Clarissa Pritchett."

"Hugh Godfrey."

He was anxious to make more contact and wondered why nothing was happening. He'd been waiting for Marion to speak. It was so long since he'd been anywhere on his own, he'd forgotten he could take the lead. Instead he'd been cringeing, waiting for the first gaffe. Marion had once heard herself described as 'pert' and taken it to be a compliment. Nerving himself Hugh began, "Speaking professionally — "

"Which is what?"

"Oh, I'm a doctor." It didn't matter now. Willoughby was the fall-guy here. "I'd say later on, Mrs Willoughby has every chance of becoming saggy."

"What an uncharitable thought!"

He'd been as crude as Marion. "What I meant to say — "

"Don't worry. I won't tell on you." She grinned, "I'd say — speaking as a female — she'd make damn sure she didn't even if it meant flogging the Gainsboroughs."

This time he laughed. "I expect you're right."

"Are they genuine?"

"The — Gainsboroughs?" he asked cautiously.

"The bosoms."

"Oh, I really couldn't say."

Clarissa looked at her hostess thoughtfully. "I wonder what she looks like without any clothes."

"Oh, yes!" said Hugh before he could stop himself. Miss Pritchett's grey eyes were very cool. "Why are you here?"

"To relax. I've had a bit of ulcer trouble. And to get away from my wife." The way she looked at him this time, he could've bitten off his tongue. He tried again. "I'm forty-five, a bit of a slob these days. I want to get fit. Toned-up physically and mentally."

"That's better."

He felt relieved. He liked this girl. "What about you? You certainly haven't come here to lose weight?"

If anything she needed to put on a few pounds. She looked back pointedly to where Jonathan was now making military noises to the Colonel. "I came to get away from that but it insisted on coming with me."

"And his mother?"

"Oh, Edith was part of the reason I came. She's had one of those hip jobs done recently and needed to get fit. Then she's going to sell her house and gamble the proceeds. She's had two unhappy marriages and the only fun she can ever remember was winning a hundred and seventy-eight pounds on Lester Piggott."

"We met outside the Consulting Room. She mentioned one or two. . . family matters."

Clarissa sighed. "Poor love. Cooped up in that ghastly Manor all day with no one to talk to, no wonder she comes out with chilling details to strangers. Unfortunately they're usually true. Jonathan does resemble his father in every possible way, which is why she loathes him and that's what keeps her going, I think. The thought of spending everything before he can get his hands on it. He's here keeping tabs on her, of course. She let slip about this holiday and that was that. Purgatory for Jonathan would be solitary confinement. Half a day of it and he'd go potty. Which is why he ensures it never happens."

Hugh nodded. Clarissa had no idea why she was talking so freely but it was very relaxing. She liked Hugh's quiet face. She knew he'd been watching her from his corner. He cleared his throat. "I had a dog once that couldn't bear to be left. Called Roger. He ate his way through a door one day when he considered I'd been away too long."

"Why Roger? It's an odd name for a dog."

"He came from Potters Bar."

This time she laughed out loud and he enjoyed it. He should have known it couldn't last.

Mrs Burg tapped on a tiny brass gong and Miss Fawcett flung open doors to the dining room. Following behind Clarissa, Hugh saw that this room had escaped restoration. Tapestries hung on the walls, rugs covered the flagstones, but Henry would have recognized this part of his castle. Half a tree smouldered in the fireplace, cocooning them with heat. Hugh sighed with pleasure.

He noticed the waitress, a breathless girl, setting another place at the top table. Jonathan had overcome his fear of Valter sufficiently, he was prepared to break bread with him and the Willoughbys. It wasn't Mrs Willoughby's attractions, Hugh felt sure. Jonathan would want to impress his hostess, not be excited by her. He now made elaborate gestures across the room to his mother. She must understand, he gesticulated, that etiquette dictated he remain where he was. Mrs Rees watched the pantomime. "We've been spared," she told Clarissa. He made one attempt to sit in the carver chair but the Colonel had come across fellows like him in the army. After a brief skirmish, Jonathan found himself sitting uncharacteristically with his back to the audience.

Mrs Arburthnot, too, was displeased. She had ended up *à deux* with Miss Brown. Miss Fawcett took in the situation at a glance and asked if she might join them. It was her duty, she knew. It enabled Mrs Arburthnot to ask all sorts of intimate details about the Willoughbys.

There was one empty table laid for two. Hugh guessed this had been intended for him and wondered who the missing guest might be. Mrs Rees waved him into Jonathan's place and he settled there happily. Smiling at Clarissa he asked, "Dare I demand a wine list, d'you think?"

The breathless girl appeared beside him. "Dr Godfrey?"

"Yes."

She put in front of him a very small glass containing a minuscule amount of cloudy liquid and prepared to leave.

"No menu?"

She looked uncomprehendingly. "You're the ulcer, aren't you? That's your dinner."

"What — all of it!"

Non-plussed, the girl glanced across at Mrs Burg for guidance. "You were quite correct, Dr Godfrey," she called "you have been prescribed — the liquid diet."

"Will it bother you, sitting with us?" asked Clarissa. "Edith and I are to have full meals."

Manfully, he shook his head. The waitress reappeared with a basket of warm wholemeal bread and delicious-looking soup. Mrs Rees tasted hers. "Mmm — lovely!"

Saliva filled Hugh's mouth. Willpower evaporated. "Surely I can have a glass of milk?" he demanded, "Dr Willoughby must have suggested it?"

"Not milk, no. We never serve it." And the waitress was off.

"Never mind," said Mrs Rees, "if you keep that up, your dressing gown might fit."

"Excuse me — Dr Godfrey?"

Hugh looked up. An earth mother was staring down at him with compassionate brown eyes. "I'm Mrs Ollerenshaw, in charge of diets at Aquitaine."

"Oh, yes?"

"I understand you have a query?"

"If you're responsible for this soup. . ." Mrs Rees was licking her spoon, child-like, "pray accept my congratulations. I would love some more." Mrs Ollerenshaw signalled to the waitress.

It was all so unfair, Hugh thought. He watched the woman pull up a chair without offering to help. He tried not to sound petulant. "I had assumed, naturally, that I would be given bland food at regular intervals."

Mrs Ollerenshaw clasped her large hands in front of her. Her white overall gaped open. Hugh glimpsed a solid pink bra. It was the sort that had hooks and eyes all down the front.

"Why should you assume bland foods, Dr Godfrey?"

"Twenty-odd years in general practice, treating others with the same complaint."

She shook her head with gentle amusement and said kindly, "But your remedies did not work, did they? Otherwise you yourself would not be here. And how many of your patients needed the knife? Here, we disapprove of cutting flesh. Or eating it. We use the old cures, the proven ones. Come, taste your drink."

He took a sip and let it swill round his mouth. His tastebuds snapped shut and all the fur on them melted. Carefully, using only the tip of his tongue, he searched out his born-again teeth. They were all still there but surely the gaps between them were wider? Shock made him swallow and it took an act of will not to regurgitate.

"What on earth's in it?"

"An extract of herbs and roots. I gather them at dawn in

31

the park."

Where the victims of the Black Death lay buried.

"Mrs Ollerenshaw, I don't doubt you have excellent results with some patients, but I must insist — " He'd gone on the wrong tack. "I would like to know, very much, what is in this brew."

She put a dusky brown hand on his arm. "Trust me. Give Nature a chance and do not, I beg, take any chemical substances while we are treating you here. They do not always. . ." She was unable to find words to describe what had happened on previous occasions but recalled something else instead.

"I have sent a hot drink up to your room. Finish it before sleeping if you wish to be healed." And she left, planting her sandals firmly on the flagstones. Mrs Rees spooned up the last of her second helping. "If the rest of the meals are as good as this, I shan't complain."

Hugh took another tentative sip. This time he was aware of all his sinus cavities. Heat spread through nose and cheekbones as soft tissue disintegrated. He blinked back the tears.

The waitress arrived with glorious platefuls of salad and the two women exclaimed with delight. "So pretty it just makes you want to eat, doesn't it?"

Hugh wondered if Willoughby was still about and whether he'd ever tackled a perforation? Probably not since hacking cadavers in medical school.

Clarissa was looking at Jonathan with narrowed eyes. He too only had a glass and was tossing off his drink with apparent enjoyment.

"The only reason he's being good," she said slowly, "is because he's got six Mars bars hidden somewhere. D'you remember him buying them at the last Service Station?"

"Oh, yes." Mrs Rees glared at the traitor. Completely oblivious, Jonathan continued to talk with great animation.

"Clarissa, why don't you nip up to his room and throw them in the moat?"

"No," she replied thoughtfully, "why don't I produce them

in front of Mrs Willoughby — and ruin his reputation?"

They laughed and for a moment Hugh too was happy, then a silver jug passed in front of his nostrils as Clarissa said casually, "Have you tried this home-made mayonnaise? It's absolutely marvellous."

Unable to bear the sight of their food any longer, he moved so that he could watch the rest of the room. Mrs Willoughby had risen to her feet. Now she rang a small bell to attract their attention.

"Ladies and gentlemen — that is the last occasion on which I shall use those words, I hope. We have met new guests and welcomed back old ones. You are now our friends and that is how Gerard and I will think of you. I hope you will regard us in the same way. . ."

Sheila Arburthnot nodded. She always liked that bit. She was poised on the edge of her chair because she knew the speech backwards and was determined to make the impromptu reply on behalf of the guests.

"Gerard and I want you, as friends, to make our home your own during your stay. We want you all to relax, unwind from the cares and tensions that have brought you here so that when you leave us next Saturday — or Sunday for those staying on for breakfast — each of you will face the world with renewed vigour, having regained your full potential as a human being. . ."

Her carefully modulated voice ceased but once again Mrs Arburthnot wasn't quick enough. Jonathan was on his feet the instant he recognized a final inflection.

"Ladies and gentlemen. . ." He raised his tiny glass, "Fellow sufferers — and those amongst us who are gorging themselves. . ." He gestured scornfully to the two salads but Mrs Rees didn't care. She kept on chewing.

"I hope I speak for all of us when I say — "

But they were never to discover whether he did or not.

Tapestry curtains billowed in a swirl of fabric that caught Jonathan off balance. He grabbed the edge of the table. Maeve pushed her way through and stood, white-faced.

33

"Does anyone round here own a dog?"

Her voice barely rose above a whisper but they all heard it. They watched in silence as she dropped a knife on the table. Blood still dripped from the blade. "I had to do it. It went for me. I had to kill it. . ."

Jonathan swallowed hard. Being upstaged was one thing, now he was genuinely afraid of being sick. The Colonel rose, staring at the knife. Hugh found him unbelievable, a puppet soldier standing regimentally straight, metal-rimmed glasses balanced on a purple nose.

"When you say 'dog', d'you mean a dog — or a bitch?" he asked. Maeve looked at him in disbelief. Unlike most of the others in the room, she had never attempted a killing before. She was still suffering from the shock which accompanies the first effort.

"I ask," the Colonel went on, "because Susie is about to whelp. Brucie has a little problem in that direction so we've had to pay enormous stud fees. . . valuable bitch, Susie. Got a brindled coat, too," he added helpfully. "So was it her, or not?" None of the discussion about British interrogation methods had prepared Maeve for this, either.

"I don't know what you're talking about."

"Oh come now. Both hounds have name-tags. . .'Brucie' and 'Susie'."

"Listen you." The sophistication she had learned in Kilkenny was fast disappearing, "I don't know if it was male, female or what. All I know is that it came for me — all teeth. So I stuck my knife in its throat over and over again till it was dead. Look at the state of me." She moved in front of the table so they could all see her jeans. There was a clatter as a fork hit the flagstones. Mrs Rees had stopped chewing. Maeve leaned across at the Colonel, "If it was your bloody dog, how come it was roaming loose like that?" The Colonel disapproved of women who swore. "Probably took you for a hitch-hiker," he said coldly.

Miss Fawcett made the mistake of stepping into the breach. "How about some carrot soup? I'm sure Mrs Ollerenshaw has

34

some left — Oh, dear!" She'd caught the full impact of Maeve's jeans for the first time. "We only use vegetables, Miss Kelly. . . It is Miss Kelly, isn't it?" she finished lamely. Maeve nodded and sank into a chair.

"Will you kindly explain where this — carnage — took place?"

The Colonel was standing by the window.

"How do I know? This is the first time I've even been in England. There were trees, that's all I can remember."

"Presumably the park." And the Colonel disappeared.

Mrs Burg came across and pointed at the rucksack.

"Can you manage that thing yourself?"

"What?"

"The man who usually does has gone home. You're in number seven." She shuffled away again. Maeve looked after her, stupefied. She'd been mad to leave Ireland! Something of her feelings communicated itself to Miss Fawcett. Had their greeting lacked warmth? "Welcome to Aquitaine," she said kindly.

On their way back to the library, Hugh offered Mrs Rees his arm. "All rather unfortunate," he ventured.

"Very." Mrs Rees was brusque. "I hope they take that knife away from her. I shan't feel safe till they do."

A voice hailed them and Jonathan hurried up. "So sorry to desert you. I've had such a fascinating evening. Valter is a lovely man."

Clarissa said in disbelief, "An hour ago you were accusing him of trying to kill you!"

"I did no such thing." Jonathan's eyes were limpid pools of innocence. "Anyway Valter explained all that. He's Dutch. He said 'Look out' meaning just that. 'Look out — at the view.' It's an absolutely wonderful view, too. I'm so glad I insisted on the second floor. The air up there is simply marvellous."

"Jonathan, how can you stand there — "

"Oh, don't be tiresome. I understood perfectly well what he meant. You didn't hear properly. You never do these days. I

35

suggest when you have your eyes tested, you ask them to check your ears as well."

"I am not having my eyes tested!" Rage made Clarissa clench her fists.

"Well you should. You squint dreadfully when you're trying to read scripts. At your age, glasses are a wise precaution, I'm sure Dr Godfrey agrees with me . . . Dr Godfrey?" But Hugh had slipped away, leaving the lovers to bill and coo.

Back in his room, he was bored. He looked at the selection of books he'd packed, and rejected them. He tried watching TV with the sound turned down, imagining the lady newsreader trying to seduce him. She didn't look as if she was enjoying it.

Eventually he sat on the half-tester bed and nerved himself to try Mrs Ollerenshaw's second potion. As he unscrewed the Thermos, the sweet smell of decay filled his nostrils but wasn't unpleasant. He dipped in a finger and tasted it. Not bad! He wanted more, half filled a glass and drank deeply. In the dying embers he could see blue, green and gold. What sort of halucinatory stuff had she put in this? He poured out the rest of it. If he felt one twinge from his gut — even the suggestion of one — he would demand milk three times a day and they could stuff old proven remedies.

The fire glowed more vividly, filling his eyeballs with beauty. He wanted to reach out and touch it but his arms were too heavy. Through the window he could hear peacocks crying out to dead souls, then silence. Hugh slept.

Below stairs, staff discussed the week's intake and made notes from Miss Fawcett's treatment chart.

"Arburthnot's back again."

"She's not!"

"And Miss Brown."

"She's all right. Still bouncing about, is she?"

"Yes. No early treatments by request because of her morning jogs."

"Yes, of course." Pencils scribbled busily.

"Have I got anyone special?" Millicent, Junoesque and

capable, was one of the two masseurs. Jessie ran her finger across the paper. "You've got some of the new people. There's a Mrs Rees with a hip who's come with an Honourable Miss Pritchett. They're both with that dreadful telly man. Wilfred's got him."

"Richard Dimbleby," the breathless girl called from beside the sink.

"I hope not. He's dead."

"Richard something, anyway. I heard Dr Willoughby say."

"He's a Mr Power and he's in number five," said Mrs Burg firmly.

"He makes those programmes about persecuted animals."

"Oh, him. . . I never watch those."

"Neither do I. Especially that one about the sheep."

"Did you hear what number seven did to Brucie?"

Heads nodded round the table. "Not the sort of thing you expect from a guest," said Millicent primly, "my lady is most upset." Most of the staff were from the village. Their memories went back before the French Revolution.

"The Colonel and I are burying him at first light." Wilfred was solemn. Jessie shook her head ruminatively.

"He was always one for a nip, was Brucie, but there was no call to do that. Have you met the party in number six, Wilf? Mr Von Tenke? Personal friend of the Colonel. Knew him out East, Miss Fawcett says. Did you ever come across him?"

The Colonel's former batman sat very still. He clasped his forearms and stared fixedly at the black hairs against the white skin as though their colour offended him. In his mind's eye he saw steamy green leaves, sunlight filtering through rattan blinds, heard that high-pitched, nasal giggle.

"No. Never heard of him," Wilfred answered.

A bell jangled on the service panel.

"She's ready for you," Millicent said fondly.

Under the bell the label read: 'Solarium'.

He put on his immaculate jacket, smoothed white duck trousers and checked his appearance in the mirror out of a desire for perfection. The same urge made him comb his sleek

37

black hair. He'd shaved twice today already but he ran a hand over his chin to be sure. Jessie gave him a pile of clean towels. He put his tray of oils on the top.

He went noiselessly along the corridor and pulled open the door. A notice hung on it: 'Solarium closed until 7.30 a.m.' Inside, lights were low except for one corner where behind glass screens a sunlamp burned. Wilfred moved down the staircase on the balls of his feet so as not to disturb the birds. Behind the screens, on the bench, Consuela lay naked except for pads over her eyes. Wilfred set out his oils, hung up his jacket then stood, waiting patiently. He gazed passively at the erotic object in front of him. A timer pinged. The ultra-violet began to fade. Consuela sat up, removing the pads.

"Good evening, Wilfred. How was your mother today?"

She stood. He flung a thick towel over the bench and she lay on it, face down. He spread a smaller covering over her wonderfully tight buttocks. As he poured oil into his cupped hand, he considered the wreck he'd tended earlier, the clouded eyes that had stared at him. His mother had taken one small step into the next world — why wouldn't she let go? He didn't want her to suffer.

"I don't think she'll last much longer, madam."

There was no hint of the daily struggle, of the strength the old woman summoned up in her fight to stay alive. Wilfred began to massage each of Consuela's perfect toes. His mother would be on her own now, terrified of the dark. No one would call at the cottage until a neighbour reluctantly took in breakfast next morning. She'd leave any mess she found for Wilfred to clean up. "It's not right," she'd say when he went round on Fridays to pay her. And Wilfred agreed. His mother had had her full span. She might have to suffer if she wouldn't let go.

He worked in silence, pausing only to pour more oil into his hands. Consuela turned on to her back, not bothering to cover herself. His strong fingers caressed and moulded each perfect curve. The tempo increased. His hands pressed harder and harder. Sweat ran in rivulets, soaking his wristbands, mingling with the bergamot oil on her body. In a frenzy he pressed down on her shoulders, ribs and thighs, squeezing and cupping the flesh, then he scraped off the excess oil with the hard edge of his fingers and stood back exhausted. Consuela rose and went slowly to the wall mirror. She and Wilfred examined every aspect of her body. In the dimness, her skin rippled like gold silk. Dissatisfied she stepped on to the scales and stared down between her magnificent breasts. Her toenails glistened like ten drops of blood. "I think I'll fast until Wednesday." He nodded. Her desire for perfection was equalled only by his own. He held out her robe. She slipped her arms into the sleeves and tied the sash. "I hope your mother doesn't become too much of a burden, Wilfred. We couldn't manage here without you."

"Thank you, madam."

She went up the stone staircase. "Goodnight."

"Goodnight, madam."

He stowed the towels and hung the rest of his clothes on a chair. He climbed up rungs bolted to the wall until he reached a high point in the dome. There he unfolded a hammock. One end was secured to the topmost rung, the other he fastened to a hook, then he swung himself into the cradle. Thick hot dampness closed round, soothing him. The acolyte had served his priestess. Now he could sleep.

Chapter Two

HUGH WOKE WITH a start. He'd been dreaming of Marion. He'd been chasing her, trying to catch her but always she'd been just ahead of him, turning to ridicule him. As he woke, she wasn't there. "Marion!"

"No. My name's Beverley."

It was the breathless girl, slamming a tray on his bedside table, knocking over the clock.

"I was dreaming."

"You feeling okay? You look peculiar."

Was this the way to encourage full potential?

"I'm feeling very well indeed."

"Your programme for the day — all the appointments and things, it's under your plate."

"Plate!" Hope sprang eternal.

"It's only got a glass on it. Liquids. We never serve breakfast. Exercises are at ten o'clock and Mrs Willoughby sent a message. She says you should swim for at least twenty minutes before then." Beverley pulled back the curtains revealing thick Yorkshire mist. "It's going to be fine later on."

Jonathan's preparations for the day had been extensive. He stood in Reception waiting for newspapers to arrive, clad in a brand new track-suit, trainers, McEnroe socks, leg warmers and a silk cravat knotted loosely at his throat. He raised a leg experimentally, rested his foot on a chair and swung one arm carelessly over his head in an effort to touch his toe. Something snapped. Was it inside his body? He could not tell. Swiftly he resumed an upright stance. Mrs Burg watched anxiously. She'd seen harm come to grown men before now. He began to breathe deeply.

"The boy will be at least another half-hour because of the fog.

Why not go back to your room and have another nap, Mr Power?"

"ZZ!" Jonathan paused in his efforts to over-oxygenate. "Can't bear to go back to bed once I'm up. Can't bear to waste a minute of my time here."

Looking at him, Mrs Burg had to agree there was room for improvement. A week scarcely seemed long enough. "You'd better carry on then."

Miss Brown appeared on her way out for a run. She had on inexpertly patched corduroys and elderly plimmers. She looked at Jonathan with undisguised admiration. "Mr Powers — I didn't realize you were an athlete as well!"

Jonathan took a deep breath and held it for a hundredth of a second. "Not really!" he exploded.

"I don't suppose you feel like jogging do you?"

"Not this morning, Miss Brown." He'd no intention of getting his new outfit dirty on the first day. "Tomorrow, perhaps."

"Super!" Joy shone out of her eyes and he felt kindly disposed.

"Where exactly do you jog to?" he asked.

"Oh, not far. I work up to it gradually." She listed the week on her stubby fingers. "Today as it's Monday, I only go round the estate. About five miles. Tomorrow I go round home farm as well. Wednesday, I get up specially early so that I can get to the far side of the moor."

Dear God, thought Jonathan, by Friday she probably takes in Scotland and Wales. "Tomorrow," he said carefully, "but only if Mrs Willoughby thinks I'm ready for it."

"Good-O. I'll ask her for you, shall I? We're old mates." She trotted off over the cobbles and down to the drawbridge, legs pumping like piston rods. Jonathan made a mental note to get to Consuela first, then, finding himself once more alone, sauntered off to the Solarium.

The gardeners had finished cleaning the pool. Fresh blue water cascaded from the topmost fountain past thick ferns, through the mouth of a dolphin and into the pool. Condensation ran down the geodetic panes and, as sunlight broke through the fog, the dome became a misty primordial cathedral, suspended in time. Jonathan felt a terrific urge to plunge into the pool but remembered in time he'd have to take everything off. He considered removing the leg warmers — it was so hot in here — but didn't want to spoil their effect.

There was a splash as Hugh ducked under the wall of glass and surfaced inside the dome. He swam towards Jonathan. "It's chilly out there this morning."

"What about the water? How's that temperature?"

"Blood heat. Swim outside, there's cold air in your lungs and warm water all round you."

"Sounds heavenly."

Hugh gulped a lungful of air and dived, leaving his legs waving about aimlessly. Jonathan thought this extremely rude. He also considered Hugh stayed down longer than was wise. When he emerged at last, Jonathan asked, "Seen anything of Clarissa this morning?"

Winded, Hugh shook his head.

"She's probably overslept, poor dear. I've been working her hard, I admit. She's looking worn out, isn't she?"

"No," said Hugh innocently, "she must be resilient."

"Oh, she is. Absolutely resilient. Almost tough, in fact." He walked away bow-legged towards the door. Beneath his leg warmers, the skin felt quite unpleasant.

Wrapped in fluffy pink towels, Mrs Rees waited for hydrotherapy. The treatment rooms must once have been the stable block, she decided. Windows high in the walls had metal grills, now softened by pink curtains. There was thick mushroom carpeting which poked between each arthritic toe. In wooden stalls there were comfortable chairs. As she waited in one of these, Mrs Rees dreamed of the time when, as a girl, she had a pony for daily rides in the paddock.

"What's Vacuage?" Maeve asked. She was studying a list.

"They do it with a rubber thing like a plunger. The same principle as unblocking a drain, I understand. They clamp it on and suck up flesh. It helps break up fatty tissue. You're not having it, surely?"

Maeve, a towel draped sarong-like round her slender body, still wearing elbow-length gloves, moved on to examine some cosmetics. "I don't believe I am, no. But I was thinking, wouldn't it hurt like hell? If you used that thing on someone who didn't need it? To suck the flesh off their bones?"

Mrs Rees was shocked. "What makes you think like that? They would never use it on a person who didn't need it!"

"If they did though." Maeve's thoughts moved on a different plane entirely. "Wouldn't it make a person scream with pain?" The girl was in a world of her own. Mrs Rees looked at her sharply. She'd employed a maid like this once, taken on solely to oblige Matron at the local institution. It had been a mistake, of course. She spoke loudly and clearly so that this Irish girl would understand. "The treatments here are supervised, the staff experienced. They will not, repeat not, do anything unless it will be beneficial and in your case Vacuage is very unlikely indeed."

"It's a thought though, isn't it?" Maeve said dreamily. She saw a Brit at her feet, writhing, as she sucked out his eyeballs. The reality and fear of last night were long gone. Mrs Rees tried to recapture the comforting memories of her youth but they refused to come back. She could only recall that the pony had eventually been taken to the knacker's yard. Had they sucked the flesh off his bones when they'd turned him into catsmeat?

Millicent stood in the doorway, trailing fragrant odours. "Your bath's ready, madam." Mrs Rees was on her feet in an instant. She'd never liked the Irish. As she went outside she didn't bother to lower her voice. "I should warn you," she said to Millicent, "that young woman is unbalanced and extremely free with her sheath knife."

The water didn't soothe. Miss Kelly had spoiled that, too. Millicent worked the hose as gently as she could over the slack sack of flesh but Mrs Rees remembered Harold. He'd certainly screamed with pain. She'd been young enough to think she could forget, but she never had. She closed her eyes and gripped the support tightly. Millicent stopped using the hose. Against the rubber cushion, Mrs Rees's face now had a greyish tinge. Dr Willoughby had warned of a weak heart. It didn't do to take risks.

At ten o'clock, Hugh descended to the lowest level of Aquitaine. Sconces in iron brackets illuminated the way. Why did they have the gymnasium in a dungeon, he wondered uneasily. He went in. Jonathan stood in the centre of the room, apparently trying to rid himself of a hand. He shook his arm violently to dislodge the article. When that failed, he began the same routine with a foot. Seeing Hugh's stare, he explained he was warming up.

Clarissa came across. "How's the diet?" Hugh patted his stomach. "Flatter already and I slept like a log. First time I've done that in months."

"Good."

She looked as if she was really pleased. Her hair was tied back with a ribbon and she wore shorts. Hugh found the whole effect delightful.

"I feel marvellous, too," Jonathan butted in, "absolutely fantastic. This place is getting through to me all the time." Neither Hugh nor Clarissa replied. Each was wondering how many Mars bars he had left.

Miss Brown hurried in, short grey hair spiky after her shower. "They're burying Brucie under the big yew. Such a pity because it's always damp there. Never mind. His master can see his dear little cross every time he stands on the terrace."

She looked at them all expectantly. Maeve said, "He went for my throat. I had to kill him."

"Oh, yes. . . Oh dear. . . Of course."

Jonathan began skipping with an imaginary rope and Miss Brown trotted over, grateful for the diversion.

"It was super out there this morning, Mr Powers. You missed a treat. When the sun came out, everywhere was lovely. Do come tomorrow. You won't forgive yourself if you don't."

"Going jogging, Jonathan?" Clarissa was unable to keep the

44

surprise out of her voice. It had happened once before, when he'd wanted to be the first at a BBC budget meeting, but he'd paid the price. He'd been unable to speak. Now, absent-mindedly, he grasped a wall bar and bent both knees. The cracks echoed like pistol shots. "I may, or I may not. It depends on Mrs Willoughby. I have placed myself unreservedly in her hands."

They were all looking at him. Too late, he realized he would have to straighten up.

Valter came in without appearing to notice any of them. Stripped, he looked like a wrestler. He grasped the pommel of the vaulting horse, swung both legs over and landed on his toes. Then he repeated the move in the other direction. Jonathan watched in a sulk. Next, Valter moved to the rings and launched himself upside down, swinging with perfect control. When he landed this time, there was applause.

"Gosh, we don't often see experts here," Miss Brown said excitedly, "Jolly good show, Mr Von Tenke."

Close to, as his skin still glistened from his massage, Clarissa had a sudden vision of Valter's hands grasping her body, and felt sick. Then the door opened again and Consuela entered.

She busied herself with a tape recorder before turning to face them. It was, Hugh thought, like watching an exotic animal. Gold glittered in her ears and round the waist of her leopard-skin leotard. Beside her, Maeve and Clarissa were insipid. She began leading them all in a simple routine when Mrs Arburth-not hurried in, full of contrition at being so late. She slipped off her wrap and Hugh saw with horror she was wearing a cheap replica of Consuela's outfit. On Mrs Arburthnot the effect was calamitous. Consuela's reaction was swift. She placed her guest in the centre of the front row facing herself. From his vantage point in the row behind, Hugh was able to make the full unhappy comparison.

On Consuela the leotard revealed the unsupported perfection of her breasts. Mrs Arburthnot's padded bra showed up equally plainly, also the roll of fat above her hips where she'd pulled in her belt too tightly. Her body stocking stretched in

45

vain over wide bony shoulders and drooping buttocks. Nude-coloured panties soon appeared. Nor could anyone miss the disparity between the two pairs of legs. Mrs Arburthnot's thickened towards the ankles and were covered in razor stubble. Her ballet slippers were size eight.

Why, oh why, thought Hugh, embarrassed. Was it a pitiful need to show admiration? Gauche worship of a goddess? Valter thought differently. He giggled and whispered in Mrs Arburthnot's ear. Hugh didn't catch all of it but as the lesson progressed and they exercised forgotten areas of their bodies, redness spread across Mrs Arburthnot's face and neck. It had never occurred to her before how obvious her attempts were to be accepted by the Willoughbys as one of themselves. But Valter Von Tenke had spotted them immediately.

Consuela kept her lesson short. She praised the women extravagantly. When it was over she indicated to Valter she would like a quiet word. Jonathan tried to engage her attention with his Achilles tendon but Mrs Willoughby wasn't interested. The reputation of her health farm depended on word of mouth. The mouths belonged to women like Sheila Arburthnot. What was the wretched Powers man saying now?

"I have placed myself unreservedly in your hands, dear lady."

"So can he come?" Miss Brown asked.

"Mmm?"

"Jogging."

"Oh, why not! What a splendid idea." Jonathan looked as if he were about to interrupt so she quickly put an arm round Miss Brown's shoulders. "You couldn't be in better hands, Mr Powers. You'll look after him for me? See that he doesn't overtax himself?" Miss Brown nodded importantly. Jonathan realized he had now less than 24 hours to think of another excuse. Damn, damn, damn — why hadn't he got in first.

Consuela and Valter disappeared. The rest went wearily to the Solarium. "Have a swim," Consuela had urged, "stop those muscles seizing up." They lay round the pool, stiffening like corpses, apart from Miss Brown. She churned up and down

46

doing her daily half-mile.

Hugh felt exhausted. The thick greenery absorbed the oxygen making him yawn. He watched as Miss Brown approached for the umpteenth time one of the two flexible plastic doors in the glass wall of the pool. Like himself she scorned to push it open but dived down the necessary few inches to continue her circuit into the open air.

Clarissa appeared beside him, and stretched out, catlike. She'd been for a steam cabinet treatment and glowed like the inside of a shell.

"What was it like?" he asked.

"Lovely. I had a Sitzbath afterwards."

"What on earth is that?"

"You sit with your bottom in icy water and your feet in a hot bath. It tones up the system."

Hugh's eyebrows shot up. "Or induces piles."

"Afterwards you are hosed down with cold water — if you have the courage."

He groaned. "Shall I live? That's all I want to know."

Smugly, she adjusted her minuscule bikini. The pinkness extended over the whole of her body and Hugh enjoyed it. It reminded him of babies. He always found handling them very satisfying.

"Is that Irish woman still hogging the sun lamp?"

He looked across at the screens. "She is."

Clarissa trailed a hand in the pool. "I wonder if she's taken those gloves off yet? She looked very odd doing exercises in them."

"Silly woman. If it's some sort of skin infection, fresh air would do it more good."

"Now, now. She's not one of your patients."

"Thank goodness." He yawned again. "Can't stand neurotic women."

"Talking of neurotics, where's Jonathan?"

"Gone to eat another Mars bar?"

Mrs Rees came down the staircase, walking stiffly. She's lost her sparkle, Hugh thought. Clarissa went to meet her. "Your

47

herbal bath doesn't seem to have done much good?"

"It might have done, dear, if I hadn't been having unpleasant thoughts. Where's Jonty?"

"We were wondering the same thing. I expect he's in his room."

Hugh pulled up one of the rattan chairs. Clarissa settled her in it gently.

"There's been a telephone call for him, from the BBC."

"Oh, bother." Clarissa was unimpressed. Jonathan always arranged to be phoned wherever he went, believing it added to his prestige. His mother too, knew about the habit.

"No, no," she insisted. "Somebody actually wanted to speak to him. They've made an appointment for Jonty to ring back."

"Oh." Whoever it was, Clarissa wasn't interested.

Jonathan bustled down the corridor, looking for Miss Fawcett. He'd had an idea for a programme — an absolute world-beater. To have one at all these days was such a rare event, he wanted to capture it on paper before it disappeared. He saw a door labelled 'office' and entered without knocking. Mrs Willoughby and Valter were in the middle of a furious argument.

"So sorry — " he began but Consuela whirled round.

"Get out!" she snapped. Jonathan was astonished. He backed away, muttering about his search. Consuela recovered quickly.

"Try the library," she suggested, "Miss Fawcett usually takes coffee in there." Beyond her, Valter smirked at him, at the unexpected outburst. Jonathan closed the door.

"My, my, my," he thought, "haven't we a nasty temper when we're roused."

Clarissa felt drowsy. She felt detached from work, from worry, most of all from Jonathan. She let Hugh carry on talking to Edith. He obviously had a way with old ladies — Edith was beginning to sound cheerful. She wondered if he had a way with younger ones. . . ? He was standing beside her.

"Come on. Your turn for the sun bed."

She followed him behind the screens.

48

"No more than five minutes with your fair skin." He set the timer.

"Whatever you say, doctor." She smiled and edged past. He could smell her perfume. She lay on her stomach.

"Would you undo me, please."

His hands were unsteady. Why should a bikini be so different from helping elderly patients disrobe in surgery? He thought of Marion's bathing costumes, one-piece, fully lined.

"Shall I switch on before I go?"

"Please."

Ultra-violet began to glow again. "I'm off for a steam cabinet. What did you say that thing was afterwards?"

"A Sitz. You can be excused if you don't feel up to it." Cheeky bitch! He felt up to anything. "See you at lunch."

When he came out of the changing room, naked except for a towel, Hugh found Miss Fawcett waiting for him.

"Dr Godfrey, could I ask a very great favour? Not for myself but for Mr Powers?"

"Yes?"

It must be unpleasant if Powers had got her to do the asking. "Jonathan — Mr Powers — has *the most* vital phone call to make this afternoon. It's essential he makes it at precisely the *right time*, when the person expecting the call will be in his office." She lowered her voice to a solemn note, "Mr Powers has to telephone the Programme Controller at the BBC."

Not God? Hugh was surprised. "And how does that affect me?"

"Could you — would you — consider changing the time of your massage?"

He appeared to ponder. He couldn't think of any reason why his body should not be pounded at 2.30 instead of 3.00 but it irritated him. He agreed but before Miss Fawcett could launch into effusive gratitude added, "Don't let Powers keep changing things, will you? I have the feeling that his life consists of one long vital phone call." She didn't respond.

"I'm sure Mr Powers wouldn't dream of making any request that was not essential," she retorted haughtily, and left.

Perhaps it was the nakedness that did it. Perhaps if she saw Jonathan clad only in a loin cloth, she would discover he, too, lacked charm.

Wilfred folded a damp flannel round his neck, tucking it in so not a wisp of moisture could escape. He pointed to a clock on the wall. "Ten minutes, sir. I shall be within call should you need me."

After a couple of minutes, Hugh was bored. There was nothing to it. Another couple and he felt uncomfortable. He tried to concentrate on what he would write on Marion's postcard.

After seven minutes, sweat poured down his back and the frames of his glasses burned red-hot. "Oy!"

The blur that was Wilfred reappeared. "Sir?"

"Take these things off, will you? Try not to remove any skin."

"Have you had enough?"

Bravely, he shook his head. Wilfred began to move away.

"I'd like one of those Sitz things afterwards."

"It's ready and waiting, sir."

He prayed his ulcer could take the strain.

As he faced the final torture, his courage almost failed.

"Not my rib-cage or stomach, right?"

The icy jet worked its way up his legs and thighs then hit his arms and chest. He gasped. Wilfred ordered him to turn round. Coldness inched down his spine. When it was over, Hugh made a remarkable discovery. "I feel marvellous."

"That is the general idea, sir. Enjoy it while it lasts."

As they converged for lunch, Hugh heard an unfamiliar sound. Mrs Arburthnot was happy to explain. "It's Dr Willoughby taking off. He's been on tenterhooks, waiting for this dreadful mist to clear."

"Oh?"

"Poor man. He was so worried he might not reach the London Clinic in time for his consultations, then tonight he's guest speaker at a BMA dinner. Such a busy schedule! Aren't we lucky he can still fit us in at Aquitaine?"

Hugh tasted bile. It hadn't been worth the agony. Not only

was he a career failure, he was now the only medical man on the premises. Suppose someone broke a leg? Or the Irish woman reveal she had Herpes? The Gods above were incredulous at such small imaginings. They were preparing a much bigger surprise.

Jonathan was already sitting beside Clarissa. Hugh joined them without waiting to be invited. "Who's this bigwig at the BBC who's chasing you?" he asked. Better let the idiot get it off his chest. He needn't listen. He'd learned that technique years ago in surgery. Jonathan began a rambling account of the hierarchy at Shepherd's Bush. Hugh winked at Clarissa.

"Sitz," she mouthed.

"And the hose," he replied, equally silently.

Mrs Rees cut through the rigmarole. "Jonty, if I have to listen to all that again, I shall move to another table." Hugh sipped his drink. Today's potion tasted sweet and tart in the same mouthful. Like life, he thought, sentimentally.

Miss Fawcett was explaining something to Mrs Burg. It was so exciting it threatened to choke her. Mr Powers had confided that, following his forthcoming telephone conversation he was bound to need an expert stenographer — one who could take dictation "At the speed of thought! My thoughts, Virginia!" She even reproduced his pauses as she repeated the breath-taking words. "They will pour forth . . . white-hot . . . in a great volcanic flow . . . Do you think you can withstand the pressure?" Mrs Burg said she thought it sounded like a busy afternoon. "He doesn't want Miss Pritchett to attempt it," Miss Fawcett continued, "because she's not very accurate. I find that surprising with her background, don't you?"

Mrs Burg sucked the last of the acid from her grapefruit. "Not really. Any fool can type. She looks fairly intelligent."

Miss Fawcett refused to be ruffled. She hugged the rest of the secret to herself. Jonathan had also hinted that he was searching for more than a mere typist. Clarissa had given all she had to offer — but it fell short of his needs. An artist could flourish only with the right companion at his side. . . This was said absent-mindedly, as he toyed with a pen. Broken phrases,

51

tumbling out, then he'd pulled himself together and given her that wonderful smile of his. "Neither of us must breathe one word of this, must we? Dear, dear Clarissa. . ." In a way she would be sorry to leave Aquitaine. After fifteen years Mrs Willoughby treated her almost like one of the family. "Almost but not quite, eh?"

It took a sensitive man to understand that. She'd told him she would have to give notice and at that, Jonathan grew quite stern. He urged her not to be precipitate.

"The best things in life are worth waiting for. Let us simply savour this moment for all the happiness it contains. . ." Then he'd asked if she could arrange for a few things to be washed and ironed, half a dozen shirts, some vests and pants, a couple of pairs of socks — life had been so hectic before his departure, the practical side had been neglected. All the same, Miss Fawcett was surprised at the number of items.

Of course they hadn't discussed an actual salary and he'd warned it couldn't be much, but she would be working with a genius! She couldn't help it — she turned round now and gave him a knowing little smile. It wasn't acknowledged. Miss Fawcett was hurt, but Jonathan, having arranged free secretarial and laundry services, had put all thought of Virginia Fawcett from his mind.

Lunch didn't take long. As he got up from the table Hugh asked, "Does anyone feel like a walk?"

"Why not," Clarissa agreed.

"We could have a look at the park. It's where they buried the victims of the Black Death."

"Definitely not to be missed."

"I've got a treatment at two thirty."

"So have I."

"Shall we skip exercises and go at four o'clock?"

"Fine."

He went, humming to himself. He'd made a date. On the massage table he remembered he hadn't yet sent Marion a postcard. He'd do that tomorrow.

*

The sky was streaked grey and gold as they set out, avoiding the dungeon where the rest prepared to rack their limbs yet again.

"Much better to get some fresh air."

"Oh, yes. Much."

"I was beginning to feel lethargic in there."

"So was I."

They fell in step, crunching through the leaves. An early frost had brought the first ones down.

"You're looking good." He didn't know whether she liked being complimented, or not. Her woollen gloves were like a schoolgirl's. Seeing them made him feel protective. He reached out to take her hand.

"Race you!" she said suddenly, and was off. He followed more leisurely. He had no wish to be out of breath; she already knew that he was forty-five. When he caught up with her, she was sitting on a log. She looked up and smiled. Cautiously, very gently, he bent down and kissed her.

Afterwards, he'd no recollection how far they'd walked, or where. He supposed they had wandered about the park. Certainly there had been trees. They'd sat, walked, and leaned against them, aware of nothing except each other. Occasionally he had said, "This is ridiculous," and she'd said "Yes" and they'd laughed. She had teased him. Once or twice, magically, she'd kissed him. As they reached the edge of the wood and realized they would have to go back, he'd taken her in his arms and kissed her as he'd never kissed anyone before. When they'd recovered she asked:

"What happens now?"

Hugh couldn't ever remember feeling so nervous, "That depends on you."

She flung an arm behind her head, her forehead creased with worry. "I'm not the type that sleeps around. I've never thought there was much pleasure in that for a woman."

Hugh tried to keep hold of chaotic thoughts. "I doubt whether there's much more in it for a man, despite the myths. That way — it's simply feeding an appetite. With you. . ." his voice threatened to wobble out of control, "with you that would

53

be an obscenity."

She stared at him, dark-eyed. "I used to love Jonathan. Ten years ago. He wasn't so vain. Some of his programmes were good then. Well. . . one or two. He cared, in those days. Work and feelings. . . they get a bit mixed up in our job."

Hugh nodded, holding his breath.

"And I didn't realize then how ruthless he was."

"Ruthless?" It wasn't a word he'd associated with Jonathan.

"Oh yes. How else could he have survived? Have you seen any of his work lately? You have to be ruthless, single-minded anyway, when you've used up what little talent you possess, in our business. These days, he seems to lose control. He's actually starting shouting at people on screen. Arguing with them. The editor's done what he can but the next series is going to look pretty dreadful."

She was retreating into her small claustrophobic world. A moment ago he had thought she was within reach.

"Do you have to go on working with him?"

"No. It's just difficult to break a habit." She focused on him. "And what about — marital infidelity?" He'd been expecting that. "Marion wants a divorce. I've been the one who's been avoiding it. Sliding away from the thought of it."

"Has she asked you for one?"

"Not in so many words. But she's always making cracks about only staying with me for the sake of the Practice. Now I shall ask her. She'll agree, I'm sure. So. . ." He hardly dared frame the question, "It really does depend on you?" She shook her head vehemently. "Sort your own problems out first. I've got enough of my own."

He was contrite, desperate to avoid losing her. "Of course. I had no business to ask you so soon. Look, how about some tea?"

"Tea!" She stared at him. Suddenly he was no longer nervous. Confidence warmed him, loosening the tense over-whelming fear. He felt relaxed, even able to smile. "It's no good me trying to sustain passion when I'm frozen. Romeo had a warm Verona night — we're in Yorkshire. And I've got an even worse problem. I'm middle-aged, girl!" It was the first time he had spoken the terrible words. They hurt. She grinned at him.

"Not quite."

"Thanks for small mercies. Anyway, as I was saying, if I'm going to have enough strength to sort out the future — our future. . . ?" She didn't contradict him.

"I've got to have a cup of tea, right?"

"Right." And she thrust her arm under his. Their feet moved automatically, in unison, past Brucie's grave out on to the lawn in full view of the castle.

"Deep breaths," she muttered, staring at the granite façade. "Do you want me to tell him?"

She shook her head. "Leave it to me. I know Jonathan."

He was so thankful, he felt guilty. "I will, if you'd rather. . ."

"No. You've got your wife to deal with."

He'd definitely have a cup of tea before tackling that. In fact, he might even have two. They didn't talk any more but walked across the stone bridge, through french windows and into the eye of a storm.

Miss Fawcett screamed as she saw them, "Where have you been! He's out of his mind! Demented!" Her first encounter with genius in the raw had unnerved her.

"Oh, there you are." Mrs Burg was standing in the hallway. "It's all right Mrs Rees," she called over her shoulder, "they're both back. I'll go and tell him."

"What is it? What's happened?" Clarissa hurried to where Edith Rees sat in one of the huge armchairs. "We've only been for a walk."

Hugh followed, Miss Fawcett, wringing her hands, beside him.

"We simply went out for some fresh air. Surely that's allowed?"

"I'm glad to see it's done you both good." Mrs Rees's eyes had a faint gleam, "I'm afraid Jonty's been sacked. That's what all this fuss is about."

"What!" Clarissa was shocked.

"That man he had to telephone this afternoon. . . ?"

55

"The Programme Controller?"

"Yes. He decided to have a look at Jonty's new series before it was transmitted, that's why he wanted Jonty to phone. He told him it wasn't even good enough for Channel Four."

"Crikey! No one's ever said that before."

"And he didn't want to hear Jonty's new idea either, just fired him."

"Oh, no." Miss Fawcett was shaking her head, "I'm sure the word 'fired' was not mentioned, nor the word 'sacked'. I would have remembered if Mr Powers had said so." Most of what he had said had certainly been a white-hot volcanic flow. She could recall every word. "And I do think it would be better if we waited for Mr Powers to explain it all himself. Although as I understand it," she continued, ignoring her own advice, "the option on his present series has been dropped and his services as a Producer are no longer required."

"Sacked," agreed Mrs Rees. "Shows you how right the *Daily Telegraph* was, doesn't it?"

Privately, Hugh thought the critic would be agreeably surprised. Miss Fawcett gave a little yelp. The victim had appeared in their midst.

"Clarissa!"

He leaned against the stonework as if he feared it might not bear the weight of his grief, one arm extended towards her. In an almost spontaneous speech, he forgave her for not being with him at the sixth hour. Hugh looked on in disgust. The condemned man had found time to change, he noticed and now sported a smoking jacket and cravat. Jonathan ignored him altogether.

Eventually Jonathan turned to Miss Fawcett, more in anger than in sorrow this time. "Virginia, I have a very serious complaint."

"Another?" She was terrified. She still hadn't recovered from the earlier cataclysm.

"I have been robbed," Jonathan said seriously. A wave of relief swept over Miss Fawcett. Only robbed!

"What have you lost?" she asked. "Guests often leave their

belongings in the treatment rooms — "

"You misunderstand. Someone has been in my room and rifled . . ." He left that word hanging in the air for a moment, "rifled my suitcase. Certain — items — are missing."

"But what? What has been taken?"

He remained uncharacteristically silent. Ten years had, however, given Clarissa an insight into his mind.

"Somebody's pinched his Mars bars," she said, and Hugh laughed.

He decided it was politic to keep out of everyone's way and arrived in the dining room late for dinner. Everyone was at table. When he saw Clarissa, he felt his heart jolt. She'd been crying. Hugh's hands curled into fists in his pockets. He raised an eyebrow but she shook her head. Glumly he realized the only vacant place was at Maeve's table where his solitary glass awaited him.

"May I join you?"

She didn't reply but he sat anyway and sipped his drink. It was the strychnine solution again. He summoned Beverley.

"Tell Mrs Ollerenshaw I'd like a word." Maeve's attention was caught. Hugh's diffidence had vanished and he looked as bad-tempered as the rest of them. The earth mother appeared.

"Yes, Dr Godfrey?"

"I find your liquid diet no longer agrees with me. My ulcer's playing up and if I continue with this. . ." He tapped the glass with a finger, "there's every danger it could get worse. Perhaps you'd be kind enough to let me have milk and bland foods instead?"

He hadn't meant to speak so loudly. Chatter died away as they all turned to listen. Mrs Ollerenshaw shook her head sadly. "You're not giving Nature a chance. Everyone must relax during their first three days, while the toxins work their way through the body, but what have you been up to, Dr Godfrey?" There was absolute silence now. Maeve stared, fascinated. Mrs Ollerenshaw went on inexorably, "You've been over-doing things haven't you? In the park?"

Dear God! Had she been out there — spying on them? While

gathering her blasted herbs?

"And now you've got a headache, haven't you?"

He nearly swooned with the pain behind his eyes.

"Haven't you?" she insisted.

"Yes!"

"So you see. . ." She rose. "No more exertion until Thursday. And no milk. We never serve it."

She turned to Maeve. "I have left a soothing balm in your room. Use it if you wish to be healed." Maeve watched sourly as she walked away. Yesterday's cream had made her itch all night. "Here," she said to Hugh, "help yourself. You're looking as sick as a pig." She pushed her basket of wholemeal bread in front of him.

"If you're sure?"

"Eat the lot. Miserable old witch!"

He bit into a roll. Manna! Maeve called to Beverley, "Hey you — we'd like some soup over here." There was menace in her tone. The girl galloped across with the tureen. Maeve ladled the contents on to a plate and pushed it across. "Get this inside you as well. It'll stop your hands shaking."

Sex, Hugh thought savagely, gulping it down. One small hour of it and he was a crumbling wreck. He felt warm liquid smother the acid in his gut. Marvellous!

"If it wasn't for my ulcer, I'd be perfectly fit — " but Maeve wasn't interested.

"Listen, are you a real doctor?" He groaned, inwardly.

"Only I've got this rash. That fool who examined me this morning was no help at all."

How could any medical man resist that appeal? Hugh swallowed the last of his soup and was preparing to make a diagnosis when there was an interruption.

The crash of a tumbler thrown on to the flagstones made everyone start. Jonathan had worked himself into yet another rage. Hunger now added to his sense of injustice. Hugh saw only Clarissa and caught his breath. Her mouth was twisted, ugly, full of pain. He had never loved anyone so much.

"Sit down, for Christ's sake!" said Maeve. He hadn't realized

58

he was on his feet.

"That idiot's been carrying on like that all afternoon. Leave him be. He'll get over it."

But Jonathan didn't want to get over it. He thumped the table so everyone would realize how badly he'd been treated. Mrs Rees said wearily, "Jonty, do be quiet. We know it wasn't Clarissa's fault."

"Of course it was!" He was so full of spleen, he wasn't going to be denied. "The whole series was her fault. She found the subjects — I simply interviewed them. But with all my expertise — no one could have made those bloody people interesting. Well, I hope she's satisfied now . . . !" It was an outrageous accusation. Clarissa sat dumbfounded, but more was to come. Jonathan hurled his final insult, "And where was she when I needed her? Out — whoring!"

As Hugh crossed the room, a voice in his head shouted. "You can't! You don't know how to fight — and if he hits you — it might perforate! You could die!" He heard Clarissa cry out, "No, Hugh — no!" but he was at their table, then he stopped. He hadn't the foggiest notion what to do next. Jonathan rose. With sickly fear Hugh saw he was eight foot tall. Strange how he hadn't noticed it before. Jonathan gloated, temper shining in his eyes, "And what d'you propose to do now, Dr Godfrey?" His words reverberated, melodramatically. Stupidly, Hugh thought of pistols at dawn, then found he was clutching his liquid diet. He chucked it in Jonathan's face. There was a hysterical scream — "My eyes! My eyes! Not — my eyes!" Jonathan sank to his knees and Miss Fawcett gave a little moan. "I doubt whether you'll go blind," Hugh heard himself say coldly, "rinse them with plenty of tepid water and ask Mrs Ollerenshaw for an antidote." He looked round for Clarissa but she'd disappeared.

He found her in the Solarium beside the pool. He held her tightly, waiting for her sobs to subside. There was a sensation of being watched but in his anxiety, Hugh ignored it. Despite the heat, Clarissa shivered uncontrollably. He found a towel and wrapped it round her. "There, there, dear love. . ."

59

"Jonathan's spoiled everything!"

He almost laughed and hugged her to him. She was over the worst.

"That's been building up for a long time, hasn't it?"

She nodded. "He's been accusing me, blaming me for lots of things but he's never gone that far before, never called me — "

He put his fingers over her mouth gently. "Don't say it. Don't think about it any more. He's a disappointed, frustrated man and he took it out on you. Forget him."

He held the kingdom of heaven on earth in his arms, even if it was a little sodden. Clarissa's eyes were swollen, the thin skin was tightly drawn across her bones.

"Please, come back to my room," she whispered.

"Now?" In this hothouse where every finger would point at them?

"Please. I don't care any more." Then, even more quietly, "I need you."

He wiped the wet off her cheeks. "If we did, think what would happen. What they'd all say. I love you so much, I don't want you to turn to me simply on the rebound — " but she brushed away his hand.

"If you do want me, really and truly, you'll come with me now. I don't need all that stuff about reasons, finer feelings . . . Come with me now and we'll take it from there. Otherwise, I'm leaving. Tonight." His grave face troubled her a little. "Hugh, I don't care what anyone else thinks. I love you."

He helped her to her feet and kissed her softly, "I love you too, girl." They walked up the steps and the door closed behind them. In the silent Solarium, someone chuckled. It wasn't a pleasant sound.

On the way she asked, "Did you hit him?"

"No," Hugh answered thankfully, "he might have hit me back."

"Oh, no. He'd have adored it if you had, then he could've played the martyr." Her hand shook so that she couldn't manage the key. He took it from her. Once inside he relocked the door. "No doubt everyone will guess what is happening but

I'd rather we didn't have visitors, wouldn't you?" She was still shaking and stood beside the fire, looking at him helplessly. Hugh piled on more logs then pulled blankets and eiderdown off the bed and heaped them on the floor.

"You're sure he hasn't spoiled things?" she asked.

"Come and get warm."

She knelt on the bedding. He pushed her down gently, uncoiling her legs. "Comfortable?" She nodded, still with her nervous shiver. Kneeling beside her he heaped the rest of the bedclothes in a nest round both of them. She held herself rigid, waiting for his next move. Firelight turned the copper colour of her dress dull gold. He found the neck fastening and untied it, lifting her slightly so the soft material fell to her waist, revealing nakedness. She began to shake again. He lowered her on to the blankets, settling himself beside her. "Lie still my love, lie still."

She lay with the fire at her back and Hugh's arms firmly round her, his shirt against her bare skin. After a while he felt the last twitchings ebb away. Her body was still. He heard a small sigh and the whisper, "Am I heavy?" Instead of answering he kissed her hard. She clung to him just as passionately. He helped her off with her clothes then pulled the covers over her while he undressed.

"I've not made love for a long time," she said nervously.

"It'll be all right," Hugh replied, with far more confidence than he felt. How long had it been for him also? He wanted to be gentle. She saw his stocky compactness and, as he reached for her under the blankets, hugged him eagerly. She laughed as he plunged inside her, "Riding your white steed!" Laughter welled up in him also and he joined to her in wild loving abandon.

They lay in a spent tangle of limbs inside their warm nest. Through their consciousness came a sudden impatient knocking. The doorknob rattled. "I know you're in there, Clarissa. I want to talk to you." Hugh felt her stiffen and half rise. He pulled her down again, rolling over on top of her, pressing against her mouth. Her arms wrapped round him.

"This is all that matters, girl. Forget everything else."

The drumming in her ears stifled all other sounds. She was

61

no longer aware of a world outside. A little later he whispered in her ear, "You're insatiable!"

"So are you, I'm glad to say!"

This time it was she who urged him on, so eager, so wanting that Hugh was swept along on a tide of joy. Above, Edwardian Willoughbys tried to avert their gaze but failed. Outside, Jonathan grew impatient but the mahogany door yielded no secrets. He gave it one final, frustrated kick.

It was too early to sleep and he was at a loose end. His mother had slammed her door on him. He himself knew he must avoid Virginia Fawcett. She had thrown herself on his bosom in the dining room with such vehemence that Jonathan became alarmed. There had to be a cooling off period, otherwise the situation could get out of hand. He had, just as publicly, bade her goodnight. So what to do now? Ahead of him he saw a familiar figure. "I say, what time are we due to go jogging tomorrow?"

Miss Brown was so immersed in her own thoughts he had to call again. This time she responded. "I usually set off about eight, Mr Powers."

He was about to protest that nine-thirty would be more civilized when he remembered he needed to get fit. After Hugh's inexplicable tantrum in the dining room, he'd explained to Mrs Willoughby how vital this was. To overcome his present life-crisis, to compete in that savage market-place they called the BBC, he — Jonathan P. Powers — needed an invigorated mind and body. Mrs Willoughby promptly reminded him of his jogging appointment, which wasn't quite what he'd had in mind, but what alternative was there? He had to fight to win back a programme slot plus a budget, otherwise the future looked bleak.

He cut across Miss Brown's description of the joys that awaited them with a world-weary, "So be it, dear lady. I will arise at dawn," and bent to kiss her hand. He saw the finger nails and decided against it. "*A toute à l'heure, mademoiselle. Bonne nuit, beaux rêves,*" he called and wandered off. If only he weren't so blessed hungry!

In her room, Miss Fawcett went over and over the events of the day, adrenalin coursing through her veins. This evening she had bathed his eyes and soothed him. She had held his hand while Mrs Ollerenshaw applied her antidotes. He had put an arm round Miss Fawcett, kissed her on the forehead and told her solemnly that, with her help, he would become a new human being.

Miss Fawcett grew incoherent at the thought of what might now be happening in number two. Disgusting. . . filthy. . . dirty! When she'd tried to express some of these feelings in the dining room, Jonathan had interrupted sharply. He was so — magnanimous! He had told everyone that Clarissa was a free agent. If she chose to throw herself away on an older man, who was he to interfere? Miss Fawcett had been a little surprised at that but Jonathan repeated sternly 'an older man'. And Hugh was a doctor! She could not find words strong enough to describe someone who might, even now, be breaking his Hippocratic oath. Miss Fawcett's incomplete knowledge of both this and the sexual act, was clouded with notions of purity and chastity. Like the chaste kiss Jonathan had given her earlier. She considered that to be a pledge, and a binding one.

In her room, Edith Rees hoped all was well. She had never known what it was to be loved. She thought she did once, when she'd met George, and rid herself of Harold. But she'd been mistaken. And it was a long time before she'd managed to get rid of George. She regarded Hugh as an interlude in Clarissa's life and hoped he was proving satisfactory. In any event, he was bound to be an improvement on Jonathan.

Miss Brown was wide awake. What a nuisance problems were, interfering with regular habits. She was fed up too, having to share a table with Mrs Arburthnot. It was the first time their visits to Aquitaine had coincided. She'd make jolly sure it was the last. Better have a word with Mrs Willoughby. She'd understand. But what to do now? She didn't like counting sheep, not while she was on a fruit and nut diet.

Someone else couldn't sleep and stared into her mirror, her thoughts in a turmoil. Would it be worth it? She laughed nervously. It was a terrible risk. The ghostly reflection laughed back silently, urging her — go on, be brave. She opened her door.

One by one the lights at Aquitaine were extinguished but only two people slumbered. In their room there was silence except for the occasional hiss from the fire where the embers were dying. Clarissa and Hugh lay, too exhausted now to reach out and touch each other.

Mrs Rees woke with a terrible thirst. Her throat was parched, her hip throbbed as it had done immediately after the operation. Nothing but hot tea would bring relief. There was no bell she could ring, nor, she was sure, anyone to answer. It was still dark. She slipped on her woollen dressing gown and fur slippers and opened her door quietly. She had no wish to disturb other guests. The rubber ferrule on her stick made hardly any sound on the coir matting. In the corridors there was just enough light for her to see where she was going.

Hugh woke with a start and remembered every detail. Was she all right? It was almost day. He examined her guiltily. He had meant to be so tender. Clarissa stirred. He lowered the blankets cautiously. Wearily, he got up and dressed then went to look outside. He couldn't decide what had woken him. He remade the bed, taking the pillows from under Clarissa's head, half-lifting, half-pulling her on to it, and tucked the covers round her. She yawned. Without opening her eyes she flung an arm round him. "What time is it?"

"Go to sleep. I'm going back to my room."

"Come to bed." She yawned again and her arm fell limply on to the eiderdown.

"Are you — okay?"

"Mmm, I love you." She was still only half awake.

He bent and kissed her. "Have a hot bath when you get up. You've probably got a few bruises."

"Mmm!" She giggled sleepily.

Hell — he'd been so worried! What was the difference in their ages? Could he cope? He could only find one shoe. Looking for the other was too much of an effort. He'd come back for it in the morning. She was fast asleep by the time he'd unlocked the door. He took a last look, too worn out to feel lust, and stumbled down the cold corridor.

He was so tired he didn't notice the line of light under his own door. Maeve sat up in bed facing him. She was naked except for her gloves and pointed a gun at him.

"My God, but haven't you taken your time."

Shock made him sit abruptly. He missed the stool and sent it clattering against the wardrobe. He landed on the floor with a jolt that jarred every bone in his body. She scrambled to the end of the bed and leaned over him, her breasts an inch above his nose. He tried to avert his eyes.

"What are you trying to do? Wake the whole castle?"

He raised both arms in surrender and his unsupported body keeled over.

"I only want you to look at me rash," she said contemptuously and began pulling off her gloves.

"But why now? And why on earth point that thing at me? Where d'you get it anyway?" It wasn't like any of those he'd seen on the walls. It was, Hugh realized fearfully, a real one.

"I've told you — I've been waiting here half the night. And never you mind where it came from, I'm glad I brought it . . ." She waved it as if admonishing him, "This place isn't safe. People wandering about . . . and a carrying-on in the room next to mine — you should've heard it. He should be ashamed. The Colonel's got it in for me, too, because of that bloody dog."

"Come back in the morning — "

"Not after waiting this long!"

"Well put your clothes back on and I'll take a look."

"Oh stop acting like a priest and get on with it!"

He lifted her arm and tried to ignore her hard brown nipples. He remembered Clarissa's tiny pink ones, how their petal softness moved his bowels with excitement. He tried to concentrate. Close to, he could see the familiar plaque shapes stretching from Maeve's elbow to the back of her hands. Even her nails were affected. Slightly interested, he examined both

65

palms. There were patches of thick dead scale on each of them. "It's only common psoriasis," he said, disappointed. "What did you think it was?"

"Common nothing. It's an allergy."

"Oh well, if you know all about it, why come bothering me."

"That other fella agreed with me this morning. He said it was an allergy."

"He would. They invent them in Harley Street. In Pinner now . . ." Hugh yawned so wide his jaw cracked painfully, "In Pinner we call it psoriasis. You've got a bad case of it, that's all."

"Well? What do I have to do for it?"

"Take those stupid gloves off for a start." He wandered about looking for his pyjamas.

"I've got to get well by the end of the week. I can't afford to stay on."

"It was a waste of money your coming here in the first place."

He pulled his shirt over his head without undoing the buttons and began unzipping his trousers. "Go back to your own room, there's a good woman. Fresh air, exercise, a dab of calamine — that's all you need. I'll take a proper look in daylight."

"I'm not leaving. It's too dangerous."

"For goodness sake — you're only in the room next door!"

He caught sight of himself in the mirror, hair standing on end, trousers at half-mast, the Englishman in love. "Go away!"

"No."

She slid beneath the bedclothes. His bedclothes. "You can bloody well get out of there because I'm getting into it." He was damned if he'd use the armchair.

"You needn't worry. I shan't touch you." Maeve's voice had a cutting edge. Angrily he pulled off his pants. Furious, he stepped into his pyjamas and in a white-hot rage he got into bed. For the second time that night he lay beside a naked woman. This time, nothing moved.

The day grew lighter. Mist formed, filling hollows and spreading a thin cover over the landscape. Wisps of it hovered above the pool, moving slightly with the lapping of the water.

Inside the dome, the dim red lights coloured everything, turning lush green black, dulling the peacocks' feathers. Outside the mist settled as moisture on the warm glass so the birds could no longer see the view, but they had something else to watch over. At the end of the pool nearest the fountain, where shallow water was sucked through filters, an object lay, sliding imperceptibly closer to the grating. It made a tiny rasping sound as it moved.

Eventually, it bumped against the side. A stream of air bubbles rose to the surface, exploding, giving up life and oxygen into the damp heat. When the last of these burst, the object lost what little buoyancy remained and sank, to lie inert on the blue and while tiles.

Jonathan tripped gaily downstairs. It was impossible to see in him now the starving creature of the previous night. What a blessing fog was! He'd been spared. He was prepared to be at his most gracious with Miss Brown. He'd taken care to dress for the jog because he didn't want her to suspect he wasn't keen. What he hadn't allowed for was her enthusiasm. She came hurrying into Reception wearing serge shorts she'd had since boarding school and listened to his objections in surprise.

"Mr Powers — it's a perfect morning! That mist will soon lift you'll see and then — all those lovely colours in the park! It'll be absolutely glorious when we come back."

"Dear lady, surely it's too dangerous? Fog can hide pot-holes. Supposing I turned my ankle? Think of my Achilles tendon!"

She brushed this aside even more vigorously. "Come along, man. We'll stick to the tracks. You follow me. I know the way."

Trying to delay a little longer, he began peeling off sweaters. She held open the door impatiently, "Mr Powers if you really want to get fit, this is the only way. And I have to be back for a treatment at nine."

Jonathan snatched a quick look at the clock. An hour! He'd planned on fifteen minutes at the most.

"Goodbye," Mrs Burg called as he went past, hugging his knees to his chest the way he'd seen athletes do before a great

67

race. "Take care, Mr Power."

Hugh woke abruptly as Jessie walked in with his tray. He was able to get the full impact of her smile then watch as it cracked and fell apart. Maeve was sitting at his dressing table amid the wreckage of his clothes. Jessie's mouth tightened into a thin line. She banged down the tray. "You're due for hydrotherapy at eight-thirty, sir." She turned to Maeve, "'Ladies' are having a sauna at nine." The door slammed behind her.

Maeve pulled a tee-shirt over her nakedness. "Calomine, you said? To stop the itch?"

He stared, brain paralysed, the art of speech not yet returned. "I'll try and let you know how I get on." She went to the door. "Did you know you snore fit to wake the dead?" she asked pityingly, and was gone.

He flung back the bedclothes and headed for the bidet. The ladies were having a sauna — that meant Maeve and Clarissa together! He had to get to her first. The phone! He tore back to the bedside table, stubbing his toe on a stool. "Miss Pritchett isn't in her room, Dr Godfrey. She collected her newspaper and went directly to the treatment rooms." He put down the receiver and grabbed his watch. Where were his glasses? Never mind. Holding it close, he made out the minute hand at twenty-five past eight. He had to shave and get downstairs. Could he do this and find Clarissa too, all in five minutes? No, he couldn't. The exertions of the night were taking their toll. His knees felt wobbly. He picked up the phone again.

"No, Dr Godfrey, there are no telephones in the treatment areas. That is where patients are supposed to relax."

He returned to the bathroom and picked up his electric razor. What if Maeve did speak to Clarissa? Hydrotherapy? Could he persuade Wilfred to hold his head under water long enough to solve all his problems?

In the Solarium, the birds still watched and waited.

"Have either of you seen Mr Von Tenke?" Miss Fawcett asked. "He was due for a steam cabinet at eight-thirty."

Hugh and Wilfred shook their heads.

68

"Oh, dear! I do wish guests would adhere to the schedule."

She fussed with bits of paper. "Could you fit him in at ten-thirty instead, Wilfred?" Wilfred nodded impassively. He would steam, massage, bathe any body that appeared in front of him. What did it matter whose, or when?

"I don't want to have to ask Mr Powers to change his nine-thirty appointment," Miss Fawcett went on, smoothing her skirt coyly, "he's had so much to endure." She was at that stage of devotion when saying the beloved's name out loud meant everything. "We must do all we can to help him through his — life crisis!" Both men were far too embarrassed to respond to this but she didn't notice. She clacked away across the floor on her high heels.

The hose played up and down Hugh's body, moulding fat in ripples. He could hear distant voices but no cries of anger. If only he could get to Clarissa first and explain. But would she believe him? Marion wouldn't. Marion! He'd nearly forgotten about her. He swallowed an involuntary groan.

A mile away in the park, Miss Brown was marking time yet again. Her legs pounded up and down, generating disapproval. Mr Powers wasn't even trying. She'd never run so slowly in her life — only covered half her normal route. He'd made no attempt to keep up.

Jonathan clung to a tree. His Harold Abrahams shorts hung dejectedly, their starch, like his energy, gone. He breathed in shallow gasps, his body begged for mercy and a haze shimmered in front of his eyes. He'd crossed an entire county, followed sheep tracks no sane animal would contemplate, at speeds faster than Superman. He'd brushed past wiry heather that concealed knife-edged boulders and flayed skin from bone. In Yorkshire he now knew that every slope led upwards and each short cut contained an emerald-green bog.

He'd tried, Christ-like, to skim the surface of the first of these. He'd spread his arms, bent his knees and run across on tip-toe, hoping it wouldn't notice he was there, but it had, and sucked him down to its heart.

A terrible syrup had bubbled through the crust releasing a foetid stench worse than any pissoir. Miss Brown heard him yelling and wondered why he stayed where he was, sinking further and further in. She realized with surprise he was waiting for her to pull him out.

The haze in front of his eyes began to thicken. He was going blind! "How . . . much . . . further?"

"Only a few hundred yards."

She tried not to sound cross but she'd missed her sauna and she jolly well wasn't going to miss exercises as well.

"Come along, Mr Powers. You've got to push your body, make it work. It's no good giving in to it all the time."

He dragged himself away from his tree. He had to keep her in sight. Supposing he fell? Would anyone find him in time? Push himself! He'd gone through the threshold of pain — he was standing at the entrance to the next world — he didn't like what he saw. "Wait for me!" he cried as the navy shorts raced away. Straddle-legged, he zig-zagged behind her across the grass.

As he crawled up the entrance steps she called cheerfully, "See you in the gym in ten minutes!"

He clung to the Reception desk. Mrs Burg turned round from her switchboard. "Are you feeling all right, Mr Power? Shouldn't you go and lie down for a while?"

How he'd love to do just that! But his room was a whole flight of stairs away and Jonathan knew he couldn't get that far. He tried to give one of his boyish smiles but spittle dribbled down his chin. "Think. . . a swim first. . ." He struggled down the corridor, clinging to suits of armour.

Inside the Solarium, humidity mingled with sweat, sticking his clothes to his body. Was anyone about? He still had double vision. To hell with it, he no longer cared! He tore them off and tumbled into the water. It closed round him like a benison. He would float until the pain eased, one toe trailing on the bottom for he had never learned to swim. His arms floated limply and water lapped his ears, conveying the tiny rasping noise.

His toe touched something sharp. He lifted his foot instinctively and began to sink. As he rolled over, he thrust out his hands to save himself but instead of bracing against tiles, they pressed against yielding flesh.

Dead eyes stared sightlessly through a visor. The helmet was fastened to the head with leather straps and one of these was buckled tightly round the corpse's neck. In that fraction of a second that Jonathan stayed motionless, a filament of blood detached itself from the mouth of the helmet and began floating towards him, like the delicate tendril of a sea-anemone. He struggled to get away from it, churning the water, and the filament tore into smaller and smaller fragments.

In that same frozen moment he'd seen what had cut his toe. The arms were clamped to the body inside a sword belt; the unsheathed weapon dragged on the bottom of the pool.

Hugh hurried along the corridor, searching for Clarissa. The sauna was over but she'd eluded him once more. She wasn't in the library. He pulled open the Solarium door and thought at first the peacocks were screaming, then saw it was Jonathan. The man was beside himself. He was trying to run away from the shallow end and when he saw Hugh, leapt towards him, out of his depth into deeper water. Hugh watched as he bobbed up and down, breaking the surface each time with frantic cries for help.

Hugh hung on to a ladder. His arm was nearly dislocated before Jonathan was out of the pool, flopping about like a landed fish. "Look!" he screamed over and over again, tugging Hugh's trouser leg, "Over there, look!" Then just as quickly he released his grip and began to vomit.

Hugh peered. At first it looked like a shadow. Then the water subsided and the shadow had a shape to it. Something rose in Hugh's throat, making his heart pound, snatching away his breath. "No!" he shouted, but the word emerged in a whisper. "Come on." He ran unsteadily round the edge, trampling across ferns and rubbery leaves, slithering into the water as he tried to get a grip under the tightly bound arms.

"Help me get him out!"

"It's no use," Jonathan paused in his misery. "He's dead. Even I can see that."

Hugh tried to lift the body out but it was too heavy. The strap kept the neck rigid, water streamed out between hinges and visor and he could see Jonathan was right. Making a super-human effort he dragged the corpse to where the tropical garden merged with the pool and let the body fall half in, half out of the water. The helmet clinked against stones.

"There's no point, is there. . . ? Kiss of life. . . ?"

Hugh shook his head. Jonathan stayed where he was, relieved he hadn't to move closer. Hugh stared at the dead face.

The sightless eyes accused him. For no reason at all he remembered another death that had come too soon but for which he'd signed the certificate. That death had brought such unspoken relief — and trust — from the living, he'd been unwilling to question it. This time he knew it would be different.

"Hadn't we better do something?"

"Yes."

Hugh moved reluctantly towards the steps. "I'll phone the police. You stop anyone else coming in."

"Hey! You can't leave me here on my own!" Jonathan seized towels in frantic haste. Hugh ignored him.

He stepped outside. The corridor was full of people now, all going in the same direction. Where were they off to? Then he remembered; exercises at ten. He saw Clarissa. She stopped in front of him, eyes sparkling. "Good morning again," she said demurely. Had she and he once made love?

"There's been an accident."

He watched the sparkle disappear, replaced by a puzzled frown, then he spotted Consuela flanked by Miss Fawcett and Mrs Arburthnot. He tried to speak directly, without alarming the others. "It's Mr Von Tenke . . . " he began, and paused.

"Have you found him?" Miss Fawcett asked brightly, "I hope you scolded him for ruining my schedule."

"No . . . we must phone the police."

"The police?" Consuela spoke first but Maeve reacted as quickly, "Why? What for?"

Hugh could think of no easy answer but the Solarium door

opened and Jonathan stalked out. He had draped himself in rose-patterned towels, beneath them his legs were grey gooseflesh. He had no inhibitions about starting a panic.

"That poor sod's been murdered."

"What! Surely you said — accident?" Consuela's eyes beseeched them but Jonathan replied scornfully, "Accident? He's been drowned. By someone with a very nasty sense of humour."

Hugh left Consuela to cope and went to Reception.

"I'm telling the Colonel first," Mrs Burg said stubbornly, "then you can phone who you like."

"Give me an outside line," Hugh insisted. She pushed in a plug. "Over there."

In the darkest corner of the hall was a booth labelled 'Incoming calls only'. As he waited to be connected, shivering in his wet clothes, Hugh remembered he had come here for the sake of his health.

The police gave clear instructions. Hugh was rebuffed to find they were given to the Colonel but he had to admit they were executed with speed and precision. By the time he returned to the Solarium, the corridor was empty and he found the Colonel standing guard over the body. Hugh slumped on a seat, overcome by weariness. The excitement had evaporated. He looked at his watch. Only ten-fifteen. A long day stretched ahead.

He glanced uneasily at the stiff military figure. Would the Colonel stand like that until someone sounded 'The Last Post'? Suddenly the Colonel broke the silence. His nose, quivering like a pointer bitch, came to rest in a direct sightline with the vomit.

"Venison?" he said, astonished. "Who's the bugger who's been eating my game pie?"

Chapter Three

IN HIS INNOCENCE Hugh was to discover a crime far worse than killing. Naïvety proved no defence. The police arrived and after a brief conversation with an efficient medical man, he was ordered to the library to join the others and await questioning. When his turn came, he found himself in a temporary office, facing a big man with prominent eyes. Instinct made him think 'Goitre?' but in the centre of the desk was his other shoe.

"I meant to go back for that this morning," Hugh observed foolishly. The big man moved it smartly out of reach. "Hugh Martyn Godfrey?" Hugh nodded. "Detective Inspector Robinson." Something about the tone made Hugh realize it was better to ignore the man's thyroid and concentrate. He saw they were all waiting for him to sit.

"This . . ." D.I. Robinson's massive hand indicated the exhibit, "was found in room number two. The Honourable Miss Pritchett's room. Would you like to tell us how it got there?"

Hugh was stunned. He hadn't known she had a title. What did that make her father? A Duke?

"Can you explain, Dr Godfrey?"

"I left it there last night."

"You spent last night with the Honourable Miss Pritchett?"

"Part of it." When were they going to ask him about the body?

"Which part, Dr Godfrey?" The inspector was leaning across the desk. Hugh could see threadlike veins in the whites of his eyes and the burst blood vessel in one of them.

"The earlier part. I left Miss Pritchett's room about the time Valter Von Tenke was killed, I would estimate, judging by rigor. When I tried to pull the body out of the pool, the arms felt rigid. Of course it's guesswork — strapped to his body like that, I couldn't do normal checks — but I'd say it's a reasonable guess he was killed four to five hours earlier. . . that's to say, between five and six . . . approximately."

He was flustered, garrulous, too high-pitched, but he flattered himself he'd got the police back on track.

"Returning to — the earlier part of the night, Dr Godfrey. . ." It was obvious which crime fascinated the inspector. The doctor had given him preliminary details about the body. Murder was at present by person or persons as yet unknown but he had an adulterer right here in front of him, "Would you care to describe what happened?"

No I bloody well wouldn't, Hugh thought indignantly.

"After dinner, I went with Miss Pritchett to her room, stayed there and left just as it was getting light. I got dressed, couldn't find one of my shoes, went back to my own room where I found Miss Kelly waiting for me. . ."

If he'd wanted to gain their full attention, he'd succeeded. Even the minion taking it down in shorthand looked up at him now. The silence was so tangible, Hugh could feel it pressing him down in his chair.

"Miss — Kelly?"

"She's one of the other guests. She was waiting for me. In bed." He was reckless, he no longer cared. They were going to hang him anyway. How stupid to assume only women were punished for adultery.

"I'm well aware who Miss Kelly is, Dr Godfrey. What I don't understand is what she was doing in your room?"

"She's got a rash. She wanted me to have a look at it."

"In bed?"

Would Clarissa even begin to understand? "She told me she'd been waiting for some time. It was psoriasis."

Diagnosis did not help Hugh now.

"When did Miss Kelly leave your room, Dr Godfrey?"

"Later."

"How much — later." There were beads of moisture along D.I. Robinson's upper lip.

"About twenty past eight. When Jessie brought in the tea."

There was an imperceptible sigh. Everyone stared at him. Did the business take longer than ten minutes? How long was the drop?

"Would you care to tell us what happened during the *second* half of last night?"

It was all so different from what he'd been expecting. "As I said, I was not anticipating finding Miss Kelly in my room. I barely knew her. I'd only spoken to her for the first time at dinner — "

"You had known her, in fact, for a few hours less than the Honourable Miss Pritchett?" They were treating him like a second Ripper!

"Miss Kelly told me at dinner about her rash. She was wearing gloves so I couldn't examine it then, and I left the room soon afterwards. . . " Hugh finished lamely.

"After an altercation between you and Mr Jonathan Powers concerning Miss Pritchett?"

"Yes. . . . Anyway, after I left Miss Pritchett and returned to my own room I found Miss Kelly sitting in bed, stark naked, with a gun."

"A — gun?"

"A black shiny thing. She said she was glad she'd brought it because Aquitaine Castle wasn't safe and the Colonel had it in for her. She'd had to kill one of his dogs. She's a bit neurotic, I think. Anyway, all she wanted me to do was to look at her rash, which I did. Made a diagnosis, put my pyjamas on, got into bed and slept until Jessie arrived with the tea."

"And where did Miss Kelly sleep?"

"In bed," Hugh admitted unhappily.

"Naked? Beside you?"

"Look — she refused to go — "

"But surely her room is the one next to yours?"

"And Von Tenke's was the one beyond that. She said she'd heard 'goings on' that frightened her — 'He should be ashamed', something like that. I think she really was scared too, not pretending."

"Are you suggesting Miss Kelly heard the murder taking place?"

"I've no idea. You'll have to ask her that yourself."

"Oh, we will, Dr Godfrey, we will. Did you yourself hear any of these 'goings on'? On your way back from the Honourable Miss Pritchett's room?"

"No. I was so shattered I doubt if I'd have heard the Last Trump." D.I. Robinson's lip curled. He couldn't win, whatever he said Hugh just could not win.

"One last question, Dr Godfrey. Have you any idea where Miss Kelly is now?"

He was ordered back to the library bursting with emotion, chiefly fear. He'd been ordered not to mention Maeve's disappearance. If she had heard and therefore knew the identity of the murderer, that person must not suspect until she was safe under police protection. He wondered if Maeve would find that much of a comfort. He doubted it. She had deliberately disappeared as soon as she knew the police had been sent for. Why? Hugh stared out at the park and moorland beyond. An inhospitable landscape in which to lie-up. The line of uniformed figures, each prodding the ground with a stick, moved in slow procession further and further away. What were they looking for? Hugh had no idea. Discussion of the actual killing had been the one topic not touched on during his interview.

Mrs Rees came back from her interview very angry indeed. "I don't know where they find types like that nowadays," she announced to the room, "but they should not be put in positions of authority." Hugh's own anger deflated. D.I. Robinson had obviously tried to bully Mrs Rees — a big mistake. He watched Clarissa settle the old lady in a chair, soothing ruffled feathers. Mrs Rees looked round for something else to attack and saw the stony-faced constable guarding them. "You can inform your — superior — I have nothing further to say. If he wants more information, he can whistle for it as far as I am concerned." She looked about for Jonathan. "Oh, there you are. He wants to see you again. You're a fool if you go."

Jonathan stopped examining his nails and smiled complacently. He had bounced back, as usual. "I found Robbie extremely easy to get on with. A bit of a rough diamond perhaps, but none the worse for that. He's a media man too, you see. And he believes in the psychological approach. We speak the same language. We can — communicate." Jonathan rested a hand lightly on the constable's shoulders, "I expect his men worship him, don't they?" and went outside.

Hugh was nauseated. So that's where all the tittle-tattle had started, why the police knew so much already. Jonathan had managed to get in first, for a chat. He should have guessed. And was the reason the killing wasn't discussed, a psychological ploy? What codswallop! He looked mournfully at Clarissa. Her interview was yet to come. If only he could warn her, but he daren't. All of them sat in silence, no one met anyone else's eye. Clarissa herself was staring at a book. He was sure she wasn't reading it. If only she would give him one comforting glance . . .

A thought popped into his head. If Maeve Kelly had heard something strange in room seven, why had Jonathan not done so in room five? He would surely have said so by now, if he had. His nature would explode with the effort of keeping a secret. So where had he been? And when and how had he eaten the Colonel's game pie? Oh yes, Hugh was beginning to feel much better. The great media man had a lot of questions to answer. All the same, Hugh couldn't persuade himself that Jonathan was the killer.

A high-pitched noise interrupted his musing. Sheila Arburthnot moved to the window. "What a relief," she called, "Dr Willoughby's arrived. He's bringing a private detective to protect our interests."

It was to save the good name of Aquitaine but Mrs Arburthnot could not be expected to know that. Following a hurried phone call from Consuela, Tom Willoughby realized their investment needed protection. He knew just the man. Quiet, discreet and Consuela mustn't judge by appearances.

During the flight north, Dr Willoughby had given his man a brief résumé of the situation as he understood it and confided his own apprehensions. "Von Tenke was a personal friend of my brother's. They met out East apparently. I've no idea when or why Gerard invited him but he's like that. Meets someone, takes a fancy . . . he's very hospitable. They're usually our sort, of course, so the other guests love it. . . Hob-nobbing with people they normally only read about in magazines." Dr Willoughby was completely unselfconscious. The hoi polloi should be encouraged to pay for the privilege of mingling. "I gather from Consuela that one or two of the guests had actually had some contact with Von Tenke when they were out East. Small world. Of course you won't find that one of them did it, not a guest." There was a limit to what someone who could afford the fees might do. "Probably find it was burglars, sent by an art expert . . . The pictures in the library are priceless. . . No doubt poor Von Tenke surprised them at it . . . Consuela said something about a helmet," he added uncertainly, then shrugged. The habits of the lower classes were not even to be guessed at.

An instrument on the panel in front of him quivered and died. "Dear me, dear me!" He twiddled unsuccessfully. "They still haven't fixed this. Can't rely on anyone these days." He looked out of the windscreen for the first time since they'd taken off and gave a sigh of relief. "What a mercy that fog's lifted. I shall have to make a visual approach . . . Might never have found the place, eh!" It was a joke but his passenger didn't think it funny.

Down below, the constable listened. The engine whine was much louder now as the Partenavia Victor circled overhead. A private detective! Robbie would have him for lunch!

Consuela Willoughby watched as the aircraft taxied to a stop and the door opened. She looked intently at the man on whom the fortune of her Health Farm might depend. He was about sixty, ungainly, with a worn tweed coat over an old-fashioned three-piece suit. He clutched the brim of his trilby and carried an old attaché case of a type once issued to civil servants. He looked vague, a little shy. She understood her brother-in-law's remark. At first sight, G. D. H. Pringle did not inspire confidence. She went forward to meet him.

The police began acting strangely. Interviewing ceased. Had they discovered something? Guests' expectations rose then fell when they found they were being ignored. Uniformed men hurried in and out, other police talked furtively into their transmitters. A car drew up then drove away again at great speed. No one was any the wiser. Mrs Burg watched it all avidly. She could've sworn she'd seen D.I. Robinson get into the car and be driven away. She asked the W.P.C. now in charge of her switchboard but was told curtly to mind her own business and join the others in the dining room. Whatever was happening, they all ate lunch impassively. They were in a capsule, deliberately kept out of touch from the world outside. Maeve's place was empty. So much for secrecy, thought Hugh. Now everyone could see she'd done a bunk. If only Clarissa would look at him, just once. . . Perhaps, if he could reach her to explain about Maeve, it would all be all right.

Jonathan was strangely silent. His mother asked sarcastically if he'd lost the power to communicate but he didn't rise to it. He was confused. He'd been in an interesting discussion with Robbie when there'd been an interruption and the whole atmosphere had changed. Jonathan had been bundled back into the library without explanation. When he'd tried to charm answers out of the constable, he'd been told to sit down and be quiet. It was quite extraordinary.

Hugh was served a hearty meal. He looked anxiously at other plates but today everyone had the same. With nothing else to occupy his mind, he began reluctantly to examine the question — who had killed Von Tenke?

He didn't bother wondering how death had happened, the post mortem would reveal that. He'd seen enough to recognize that the body would need a thorough investigation, but who had been physically capable of tackling such an athlete? Apart from Miss Fawcett, Mrs Rees and Mrs Burg, he could hardly describe the rest as frail, but Valter had been a powerful man. And what was most disturbing of all was the apparent lack of motive. Jonathan's early claim that Von Tenke had tried to murder him was probably hot air, no doubt Mrs Arburthnot found the business in the gym distasteful — but to drown a man for it? It was too improbable. Hugh's brain began to whirl. He saw that Mrs Arburthnot was looking at him then she spoke to Miss Brown and both women stared. Good grief! Surely they didn't suspect that he . . . ?

Hugh attacked his salad. He needed sustenance. Something else was niggling at the back of his mind like a toothache. Marion. The longer he delayed, the worse it became. Until this morning, he'd only wanted to discuss divorce. Now there was murder, too. And what about a solicitor? The only one he knew was the man who had dealt with the house purchase, and he'd made a botch of the conveyancing. What would he be like with adultery, let alone a capital offence? His ulcer tweaked. Was it less than twelve hours since he believed himself the happiest of men?

Jonathan emerged from his reverie to pass Clarissa the salt. "I recognized Robbie when I went back for my interview," he said, absently.

"Oh yes?" Clarissa answered but the rest were listening.

"He confirmed it when I asked him, of course. He appeared on the box when he caught that rapist last year, don't you remember?"

Instantly there flashed on Hugh's inner eye TV images of D.I. Robinson leading an investigation, interrupting interviewers loudly, pointing a huge finger at the spot where the 'incident' took place and, finally, gloating over an item of underwear. There was another recollection too, far more worrying than the rest. "Here — wasn't he the officer who made a mistake?" Hugh blurted out. "Don't any of you remember that?" He looked at them anxiously. "Robinson arrested the wrong man. They had to release him from prison and the Queen gave him a pardon."

Jonathan treated this outburst with the utmost contempt. "And which of us is without sin, Dr Godfrey? Are we all to believe that you have never made a wrong diagnosis? Never

81

killed one of your patients?"

It was an outrageous suggestion. Hugh was speechless. All the same who had Jonathan been talking to? He had returned to his audience. "Robbie believes in reconstructing a crime," he was saying grandly, "as I do myself, of course. All part of the psychological process. We are all, therefore, to re-enact down to the last detail, what took place here last night. From the beginning . . . to the end." There was a hush.

"And which of us is to be Von Tenke?" Hugh asked angrily. "Because I'm blowed if I'm going to get into that pool in a helmet — "

"I imagine it will take you all your energies to re-enact your own movements," answered Jonathan spitefully. "At Robbie's suggestion, I shall retrace my swim of course."

"What about your little run?" asked his mother. "Are you going to retrace that, too?"

Hugh looked up. Consuela was beside him. Would he be willing to meet the private detective they had engaged? Hugh had no idea whether he could refuse or not, but agreed. She led the way. There was a difference in his hostess and he tried to analyse it. Less make-up? A different style of dress? Suddenly he realized — she was afraid. Why? The contagion spread to him and he had to brace himself before entering the room. Inside, a mild-mannered man rose from behind a desk, introduced himself and apologized over half-rimmed glasses for interrupting Hugh's health cure. Hugh wondered if he'd heard aright. As they shook hands he saw inside an attaché case, buff-coloured envelopes that looked familiar and made him unaccountably uneasy. Protruding from them were home-made forms. Mr Pringle unscrewed a calligrapher's pen and handed Hugh a biro. "If you would be so kind, Dr Godfrey. A few questions. And I will make notes."

Hugh read the list. Date of birth, address, occupation, marital status, family, details of parentage. It looked harmless but he couldn't understand the relevance.

"The police asked us for some of these details. Don't they give you a copy?"

"Oh no, I'm afraid not!" A tiny smile dared to appear beneath Mr Pringle's moustache but was quickly suppressed. "They regard people such as myself as a form of er, amateur. . . interference, if you like. On this occasion of course, a total embarrassment."

Hugh looked at him curiously.

"Do I take it, Dr Godfrey, that you have not yet heard?"

"Heard what?"

"That Detective Inspector Robinson has been removed from the case."

"What!"

"There has been some question of er, an accusation . . . concerning false charges. From one who has — as they say — turned Queen's evidence. He has accused the Inspector of accepting bribes. . ." Realization was slow but sure. A smile broke out on Hugh's face.

"Bent?" he said happily.

"As I understand it, Detective Inspector Robinson is assisting the police with their enquiries."

Hugh nearly cheered. So Robbie was facing an inquisition even tougher than his own. Oh glory, glory! There was justice in this world after all. "How can I help you?" he asked, expansively.

Half an hour later Mr Pringle read back his notes. "Is my record reasonably correct?"

Hugh nodded. "In every respect. I'm sorry I can't be more exact about the time of death."

"No matter, Dr Godfrey. Your estimate is sufficient for the present, until I discover whether four to six a.m. is a critical period for er . . . anyone. You yourself must be relieved to have two alibis. Once Miss Kelly has been found you will, of course, be entirely in the clear."

Hugh felt a slight hollowness at the implication. He wondered yet again what had happened to Maeve. Something else worried him. "About last night."

"Yes?"

"I haven't yet had an opportunity to speak to Miss Pritchett. To explain — subsequent events — concerning Miss Kelly."

"Ah . . ."

He could see that Mr Pringle did not envy him.

"So if when you come to interview Miss Pritchett — "

"You may rely on me, Dr Godfrey."

Strangely enough, Hugh was sure he could.

Mr Pringle cleared his throat and gave a little cough.

"I have to confess I was relieved to discover the body had already been removed. And that you — a medical man — were one of the principal witnesses. You have described the, er. . . details, without my having to. . . view. I have never been able to deduce anything from a corpse because I have always felt far too unwell."

Hugh looked at him blankly.

"I have no medical training you see," Mr Pringle explained, "and I am always far more interested in who the people were. That usually tells me more about them than the way they actually died. I have, as yet, very little experience in this field. This is only my fourth, er. . . killing."

"I see. Well, I'm afraid there's very little I can tell you about Valter Von Tenke as a person."

"You've been most helpful, Dr Godfrey. I expect to glean much from the Colonel about his friend."

Mr Pringle appeared to be in no hurry and was anxious to make his position perfectly clear. "Since taking up this work, I have, as I said, been concerned with three other deaths. Two were a supposed suicide pact — also, very messy. The other was reasonably intact. This morning, I doubt whether I could have faced . . . I'm a bad air traveller too, you see."

Hugh did. "Is there any other medical information. . . ?"

"In your opinion was Mr Von Tenke dead before he entered the water?"

"Difficult to say, I think more likely unconscious. The strap round his neck was very tight. It could've choked him."

"Or he could have been killed in some other way and the strap fastened to make it look like that?"

"Ye-es . . ."

"You have reservations?"

"I keep remembering what a big, powerful man he was. An athlete. The way he'd been trussed up . . ." Hugh couldn't find words, "It was obscene, the way he looked."

Mr Pringle nodded seriously, and turned over a page in his notebook.

"I have been informed of Miss Kelly's disappearance and that she was armed with both a gun and a knife. Detective Inspector Robinson had quite made up his mind about her apparently, and instigated a full police search."

Hugh shook his head emphatically. Buckingham Palace would be spared further embarrassment. "I'm sure she didn't do it. She may have heard it being done — I told you what she said — but she was with me at the relevant time."

"Yes of course, Dr Godfrey."

Hugh felt anxiety rising. Had he lost his only ally?

"Listen, you do believe me, don't you? I mean, why would I lie?" For Mr Pringle, this was a very serious question indeed.

"Dr Godfrey, I mentioned before that I have been pursuing my present occupation only a short time. During that period my speciality has been fraud. Figures fascinate me. You see, for most of my life I was one of Her Majesty's Inspectors of Taxes. . ."

Hugh tried to keep an amiable expression pinned to his lips.

"Now to answer your question: during thirty-odd years in the Inspectorate, I never once met a man or woman who did not lie. I have stories of horses that fell at the last fence, of men who disappeared taking all the profit with them, of speculations that failed. Never in all that time did I hear a success story. And sometimes I would go to my window (my office was in a prefab installed in the car park as a temporary measure at the end of the last war) to watch these unfortunates drive away. Do you know that nearly every one of them did so in a three-litre car?

"As to why they told me lies, I will explain: it was to prevent me discovering the truth. But I always have discovered it, in the end. Several times I have been unable to prove it. Once, when I

85

handed my notes over to the police, they were able to complete the work.

"It may be today I have listened to the truth. If that is the case, believe me Dr Godfrey, I shall regard it as a privilege, but you must realize that thirty-six years of prevarication tends to colour a man's judgement."

"I'm sure it must."

"Pray do not allow yourself to be uneasy. It is still my maxim, unlike the Constabulary, to assume a man innocent until I prove otherwise."

Mr Pringle's brown eyes were earnest and sincere. Hugh cheered up a little. Perhaps Clarissa would visit him in prison.

"I wonder you can bear to carry on, listening to lies?"

"Ah well, you see. I have a little weakness!"

G. D. H. Pringle blushed. Hugh thought involuntarily, "At his age!"

"I am a collector."

Hugh was suitably humbled. "Antiques?" he asked.

"Art. In a small way, of course. The early Manchester school. I have two Adolphe Valette's and a Lowry, painted before he turned commercial."

Hugh tried to visualize such a treasure but failed.

"Art has been a great consolation," Mr Pringle looked almost happy, "but my pension, although index-linked, does not allow for it, which is why I follow my present part-time occupation. I have had a certain success with figures. Solving a fraud can be very satisfying."

"What about the three killings? Did you have any success with those?"

"Oh, yes. Indeed yes!" Mr Pringle looked pained. "Compared to most fraud they were crudely planned. Murders often are, you know, unlike popular fiction on the subject. The victims in the three cases I have described were all former patients of Dr Willoughby, which is how he and I came to be acquainted."

How sensible to remain in Pinner where patients died of natural causes, or so Hugh wrote on their death certificates. He rose to leave. As he did so, Mr Pringle asked, "When Mr Powers broke the news, how did everyone react?"

Hugh thought about it. "Someone screamed. Millicent, I think. There was a bit of shouting. Miss Brown was quite near me, she said 'how extraordinary', something like that. Miss Pritchett spoke but I didn't quite catch what she said — and Mrs Willoughby asked me if it wasn't an accident."

"What about Mr Powers himself? You saw him in the pool. Was his display of shock genuine, in your opinion?"

"Yes," said Hugh glumly, "for once I think it was."

"Thank you, Dr Godfrey."

If Maeve didn't turn up, Hugh realized suddenly, life might become extremely awkward.

After Hugh had gone, Mr Pringle studied his form. The answers were straightforward: childhood spent in Hatch End, father a G.P., a medical degree from Newcastle University and, apart from a two year secondment to a hospital in Northern Australia, a placid existence in Pinner. No children. Wife: Marion. Hugh had added in brackets: (former S.R.N.). In answer to the final question — 'Did you know the deceased?' — Hugh had written, 'Prior to visiting Aquitaine, No,' but Mr Pringle was accustomed to prevarication.

By late afternoon, the routine police work was complete. The pool had been drained, frogmen were exploring the moat — no one quite knew why. Guests were told they could return to their rooms. "Unfortunately the fires have not yet been re-lit," Mrs Burg announced, "so if you could all wait a little longer. . ." The minibus bringing cleaning women and gardeners from the village was finally admitted. There was a bustling in the corridors, baskets of logs carted up the stairs. The guests drifted about aimlessly. The Solarium was still out of bounds. Hugh caught Clarissa by the arm. "Come for a walk, please!"

"It's freezing. I don't suppose they'd allow it."

"We've got to talk. If we promise to walk where they can see us. . ."

"All right. I'll get my coat."

87

They were restricted to a circuit of the croquet lawn. There was no sun now, nothing but a leaden sky. Round and round, under the watchful eye of a W.P.C. on the terrace. Though they conversed quietly, the sounds carried in the still air.

She shivered. "It's terrible, isn't it? Have you ever been involved in anything like it before?"

"Pinner isn't renowned for its crime figures — "

"Hugh, was he unconscious? You know, before he was. . . ?"

"Dumped in the pool? I'm not sure but I think so. I think he drowned before coming to — "

She shuddered.

"Look, love — try not to think about it."

"Don't be stupid." She looked at him incredulously. "As if any of us are thinking of anything else!" They completed another circuit in silence.

"Aren't you going to tell me about your visitor?"

He was stunned. "How on earth . . . ? Did she tell you herself?"

"How could she? She disappeared the moment you mentioned the police. Didn't you see her go?"

He shook his head.

"Poor Hugh. First you're a murderer, then a guest you seduced disappears — "

"Murderer!"

"You're the prime suspect, didn't you know?"

"Who says so?" To hell with sex. This was serious.

"Jonathan of course. While you were with the detective he told everyone in the dining room it couldn't possibly be anyone else — "

"But what reason could I possibly have — "

"Jonathan doesn't look for reasons! You should know that by now. It was some old film plot he'd remembered where there was this mad doctor — "

"Listen!" He seized both her shoulders and spun her to face him, "I've just been exonerating him! I told that detective he couldn't possibly have done it."

She tried to laugh but her top lip was frozen. Tears of

exasperation stood in her eyes, "Don't expect gratitude, Hugh, for heaven's sake. Jonathan's spent most of his adult life blaming other people. It's a survival instinct — the best form of defence."

"Did anyone actually believe him?"

She paused just a bit too long.

"They did, didn't they!"

"The Arburthnot woman made a fuss about it — claimed Jonathan must be right because as he didn't do it, and quite obviously the Colonel didn't, you were the only other man on the premises. She's got it in for you because of the way you look at her."

"I find her pathetic."

"Well, it shows. You should hide your feelings occasionally. Tell me about Maeve Kelly."

They were like two strangers. He let go his hold and could feel her slipping away. His thoughts were leaden so that he couldn't help himself. "I still don't understand how you found out?"

"Jessie told Millicent. I overheard. Simple. Now I want to hear your version."

He thrust his hands in his pockets and stood deliberately apart. "When I got back she was there in bed waiting for me. She had a gun — pointed at the door — I walked straight in. She told me she wanted me to examine her rash. I told her what to do about it — she refused to go. So I got into bed and went to sleep. Nothing — repeat nothing — happened. All right?"

She didn't even look at him. She stared into the distance without seeing. "Why on earth carry a gun?"

"She said this place wasn't safe. Well, she was certainly right about that." He didn't want to talk about it any more. He wanted to tell Clarissa he loved her, to get back to the magical way it had been between them. Instead, he said: "Is your father a Duke?"

"No. Why?"

"That bent policeman. Kept referring to you as 'The Honourable Miss Pritchett'."

"Oh . . . Jonathan filled in the register. I never use it but he loves that sort of thing."

She hugged herself against the cold, rubbing her arms, "Why didn't you tell me before? About Maeve Kelly?"

"Give us a chance! First there was that little matter of a body in the pool this morning — "

"There's been heaps of time since then. You just didn't try."

It was the same accusation Marion always made. He put things off. He never did anything that could be left till tomorrow. Now Clarissa was saying it in exactly the same tone Marion always used. He was so full of despair it numbed his brain.

"Come on," he muttered, "we'd better go back inside."

Clarissa didn't move. "Who do you think did it?"

"I've honestly no idea. Apart from the Colonel, I don't think anyone liked him."

"There's an awful lot of difference between not liking someone and killing them, even at the BBC."

"Yes, but I can't see how any of them managed it — he was such a strong, healthy bloke."

"Well, somebody did. And the police obviously think it was one of us." Clarissa looked towards the castle, "Mrs Willoughby's afraid. . ." She was momentarily distracted by the dark granite shape. "Why on earth would anyone build a place like that for his wife?"

"I understand it was an unhappy marriage," Hugh said carefully. "But what makes you think Mrs Willoughby is frightened?"

"I was watching her during lunch. The Colonel spoke to her once and she nearly jumped out of her seat."

"Well, she's not the only one. I'm scared bloody stiff because I didn't do it, despite what anyone says, which means there's a killer at large. Clarissa, promise you won't do anything daft like be on your own. Why not sleep with Mrs Rees tonight? Is hers a twin-bedded room?"

"There's a couch." She looked at him speculatively.

"No, I'm not coming to your room tonight, nor for the rest of our stay here. I'm waiting till we're out of this whole mess and you invite me on your own terms. I'll be waiting for that invitation, never fear. In fact, I'll be living every moment of the day, praying that you still love me. . ."

She stared, eyes big in her face. He made no move towards her. "I'm worried about Mrs Rees, too," he said softly. "It's that heart of hers."

"Yes, of course. She shouldn't be left on her own. I'm sure she'll let me move in. What about you?"

"I shall bolt and bar my door and hide in the wardrobe. Alternatively I might move in with Miss Kelly, when she returns. She's got a nice shiny gun and I'm sure she'll let me share her bed."

"You do that and I'll chop your balls off!"

He grinned. It stretched his frozen face and then he threw back his head and laughed. "Oh, I love you, girl!" His arms enveloped her in a bear-hug and he jigged her round on the spot. "Come on! Let's go and get some tea." Arms tightly round each other, they walked companionably up the steps.

"I wonder if Jonathan's managed to phone the Press. He was straining every muscle but the Fuzz have him taped. I don't think he'll beat them."

"You don't mean . . ." Hugh's whole being shied away from publicity. Clarissa looked at his shocked face and laughed.

"You don't know much about being a freelance, do you Hugh? If Jonathan managed to get himself featured in the *Sun* — it'd be worth gold, especially after what happened to him yesterday."

"But a man has been murdered!"

Clarissa shrugged.

"How did — the Fuzz — treat you, by the way?" he asked.

"A bit rude, but they stuck to the rules. A title helps, especially in the provinces." The social chasm yawned deeply. "Why? Did you get roasted?"

"Not particularly." With D.I. Robinson removed, he could brazen it out. "Most of the time they only wanted to know what went on in your room, not about Von Tenke — "

"My God — I hope you didn't tell them?"

"What d'you take me for? Anyway they lost interest in you when I told them Maeve Kelly was naked — "

"*She was what?*"

"Clarissa . . ." They were at the top step now. The W.P.C. could hear every word but he didn't care.. "I have seen more naked bodies than a dog's had breakfasts. Last night, one body — yours — gave me more excitement than I thought possible. For the first time in my life I knew what all the poets meant. . . why men kill each other for it — everything! I lost myself in you — don't you understand. I now know what it is — to love. . . And I'm quite prepared, in front of this witness, to describe all the other delightful sensations you conjured up — "

"No, no." Clarissa was bright red and moved swiftly towards the door.

"Another time, perhaps," said Hugh to the W.P.C. but she preferred horses to men, and stared through him stonily.

Once inside, he took Clarissa in his arms and kissed her cold nose. "Have you been to see the detective yet?"

"No, but I have an appointment. Look." She pulled out of her pocket one of the buff envelopes. Mr Pringle had recycled it from Her Majesty's Service to Clarissa. Inside on one of his forms he'd written, 'May I request an interview at 5.15 p.m. Yrs. faithfully, G. D. H. Pringle.'

"He's harmless," Hugh told her, "but don't tell him if you've ever diddled the Income Tax. That really upsets him."

Mr Pringle was in fact running a little late but he didn't mind. Miss Brown was proving interesting.

"Do you know anything about money?" she'd asked.

"I have spent the greater part of my life making assessments of it."

"Have you really? How awful."

Mr Pringle concealed his chagrin.

"Daddy could never cope with it."

"Oh . . . ?" He thought they were nearly there. He sat, patiently.

"Daddy always said it wasn't his fault, what happened, but it was because he trusted people. That's what they said at the enquiry. Someone else was actually responsible. . ."

"And this has to do with Mr Von Tenke?"

"Oh, yes."

"Suppose you tell me what happened?"

"It was a piece of paper which a fellow had signed as security for a loan which wasn't due for a bit but they foreclosed or something, anyway the fellow needed the money and the paper should have been safe as houses, so Daddy used club funds, which he shouldn't have done of course but he did, and admitted he had at the enquiry because he was an officer, but unfortunately the other fellow wasn't, nor was he a gent — which Daddy certainly hadn't known — otherwise he'd never have got involved but the other fellow had been in such a hole, and Daddy was in charge while the treasurer was on furlough, and the other fellow assured Daddy that a chap who owed *him* money would fork out on a certain date, but he didn't although *he* claimed afterwards that he had — but when the treasurer got back the funds were still short. The other fellow let Daddy down well and truly then because while Daddy was owning up at the enquiry, the other fellow stayed at home and hanged himself, which meant Daddy had to face the music on his own. When they heard what he'd done the chairman of the enquiry — who was one of Daddy's fellow officers — said it showed the other fellow lacked guts and this was well-known because his wife ran up enormous bills and he'd never been able to stop her." Miss Brown finished triumphantly and looked at Mr Pringle. He disentangled it.

"Your father, an officer, lent money to a civilian who firmly believed money owing to him would be repaid. It wasn't — or so it appeared — and your father's misuse of funds came to light?"

"And there was an enquiry," Miss Brown nodded vigorously. "Daddy wasn't cashiered, anything like that because he'd owned up, but he was reprimanded and that made him ill. He was invalided home."

93

"How very unfortunate."

"Then he died. He never really recovered. The shock, you know. He loved Singapore, the life out there. He kept saying England wasn't the same because of the socialists — and he was on half-pay so things were jolly tight. It was a blessing when I inherited the trust money. It's not much because of inflation but we only had the interest from it while Daddy was alive."

"And Mr Von Tenke?"

"Oh, he was the chap that owed Eric — the other fellow — the money. Valter was away when it all happened but he insisted afterwards that he'd sent Eric a cheque. At the time, Eric swore black and blue that he hadn't received one — but it was all very odd because Valter's cheque eventually turned up. It had been circulating for months. They often do out East, you know, British cheques anyway, instead of real money."

Mr Pringle pursed his lips, well aware what the treasury thought of such practices.

"Anyway Eric hanged himself, his wife disappeared and we'd nearly forgotten about it when Valter came back, swore he'd sent that cheque and told all of us what *he'd* known for years — that Eric wasn't properly married! That's when everyone decided it must have been the real reason behind it, why Eric hanged himself and she ran away, don't you think?"

"I really couldn't say . . ." Mr Pringle was lost but didn't want to stop the flow.

"She wasn't his wife, you see. Eric had married very young and never divorced — and Valter knew about it. We were all a bit surprised because they were so alike, Eric and Sheila. It was difficult to imagine him with anyone else."

"Sheila?"

"Eric's number two. They were always pretending they were upper class, poor things. She's still the same now . . ." Miss Brown looked at Mr Pringle expectantly.

"Is she?" He was beginning to lose interest.

"Always copying Mrs Willoughby, trying to make out she's one of Us. She never will be, of course. . . "

The name struck a chord. He looked at the list of guests

supplied by Miss Fawcett. "Mrs — Sheila Arburthnot?"

"That's right. One should feel sorry but I don't. She's such a bore!"

Mr Pringle examined Miss Brown in his mild, self-effacing way. Her ancient skirt was so baggy it drooped front and back, her aertex shirt had a hole under the arm, she'd surely cut that spikey hair herself? But whatever else could be said about Miss Brown, she would never be mistaken for one of the lower orders.

"Quite honestly I wasn't expecting to see either of them again. I was a bit fed up when I found them both here. Mrs Willoughby explained. . . she'd hadn't known Valter was coming herself until a fortnight ago. The Colonel, you know, awfully sweet but frightfully impulsive. And she's promised to let me know if Mrs A's booked in when next I write, so that it can't happen again." Miss Brown beamed at Mr Pringle. "She told me she finds her just as big a bore as I do but she can't turn good money away can she? Not with all that dry rot!" Miss Brown looked up at the ceiling as if expecting its imminent collapse.

Mr Pringle concentrated on the immediate problem. "Do *you* think Mrs Sheila Arburthnot knew she was bigamously married? And that was why she disappeared?"

"I don't know. She could be certain she wouldn't be invited to any of the officers' parties again after Eric died like that. Parties meant an awful lot to Sheila, she's such a social climber you see, but there were money troubles afterwards. She left a lot of debts. The only thing I do know is that she was in Valter's room last night."

He was alert now. "What makes you so sure?"

"I wanted to see him, to discuss something. Nothing to do with his being killed, just something personal. I went up to his room but outside I could smell her scent — it's a frightfully niffy variety."

Mr Pringle nodded. Cloying was perhaps the word he'd have chosen.

"Anyway I'd written a note . . . It was very late, well after midnight and I thought if the light's on he's awake and I'll

95

knock, but if it isn't he's asleep so I'll push the note under his door and discuss it with him in the morning. Only I didn't because he was dead."

"And was the light on? Did you notice?"

Miss Brown frowned. "I can't honestly be sure. The smell was so strong I didn't bother to look. I just shoved the thing under the door and went back to my room."

"I see . . ." Mr Pringle sat lost in thought. Miss Brown fidgeted.

"The thing is . . ."

"Yes, Miss Brown?"

"Could you get my note back? The police won't have read it because I marked it 'Personal' but I'd rather it wasn't left lying about."

Could anyone be so naïve, Mr Pringle wondered? "I take it you have not so far mentioned these matters to the police?"

"No, I haven't! That man was so awfully rude I didn't tell him anything. When I heard you were here to protect our interests, well. . . " Her eyes were guileless. Mr Pringle shifted uncomfortably, "I'm afraid it may be my duty to divulge facts, should they become relevant, to whoever is sent to replace Detective Inspector Robinson."

"Will it really? Oh, bother. . ." This time Miss Brown's frown screwed up her face in a hideous grimace, "Botheration!" She rubbed her hand fiercely down the side of the well-worn skirt.

"Well, do what you can to get my note back, please. I went up there myself but one of those constables ordered me to go away — "

"It is standard practice, Miss Brown, during an investigation for murder. May I ask, er . . . the subject matter? Of the note?"

This time she hesitated. "It was to do with Daddy," she said finally.

"Thank you. I will do the best I can."

When Hugh and Clarissa walked into the library they were greeted with happy chatter. Sparkling wine flowed instead of camomile. Consuela's business instincts were working well. She joked openly about the reason for D.I. Robinson's departure, her guests joined in the fun, anything to forget, however temporarily, the stigma of murder that hung over all of them. Mrs Arburthnot was particularly shrill.

Jessie and Wilfred circulated with well-wrapped bottles. On empty stomachs, it worked wonders. Millicent and Mrs Burg sat at the great oak table filling out tomorrow's treatment chart and Consuela herself handed out appointment cards with her most charming smile. It was business as usual.

From the doorway, Hugh spied Jonathan. Memory still seethed at his unjust accusation. With Clarissa at his side, he felt an infantile urge to prove himself macho. He ignored the voice inside that yelled "No!" and strode across the room, cutting a swathe through the chatter.

Jonathan affected not to notice until Hugh stood in front of him, then moved his glass pointedly out of reach. "Oh, not again Dr Godfrey, surely?" he said languidly. "Champagne makes the eyes sparkle but it has to be taken internally, you know." Miss Fawcett gave a happy yelp and Jonathan turned to give a graceful acknowledgement. Hugh grasped his arm. This time Jonathan was petulant, "I think you should realize that I'm still 'in shock'. The effects of this morning's exertions, no doubt."

"No, you're not. I'm a G.P., remember. One of the world's experts at spotting a malingerer. If you're feeling poorly, it's because you've been stuffing yourself with Mars bars ever since we got here — "

"Only four!"

"And some time last night you nicked the Colonel's game pie."

Jonathan drew breath, prepared to bluster, but Hugh hurried on, "You vomited it up when you saw Von Tenke's body. The Colonel spotted the mess and knew what it was. You must've eaten it during the early hours to regurgitate it in that state — which probably means you weren't in your room part of the time. Have you admitted that to the police?"

Jonathan didn't reply.

"So . . ." Hugh poked a threatening finger at him, "if I hear you've been accusing *me* of being a murderer — I'll — I'll strangle you!" It was an unfortunate conclusion.

"That's how Valter Von Tenke was murdered!" shrilled Mrs Arburthnot.

"Oh was he?" said Hugh coldly. "I didn't know that and I actually handled the body." Sheila Arburthnot's mouth hung open slackly. Hugh looked round the silent room. He'd really flattened the Méthode Champenoise this time, he could see that. "And if anyone else feels like making wild accusations, perhaps this is the moment to warn them they'll hear from my solicitor."

My God, that would shake the bloke up. Forget conveyancing, now there was divorce, murder and slander! What would the bill be like for that little lot?

An apologetic cough made them look towards the door. "So sorry to interrupt," said Mr Pringle, "but is Miss Pritchett here and if so, might I request a few moments of her time?"

Mrs Rees welcomed Clarissa's suggestion with pathetic eagerness. "I was dreading having to spend the night on my own. You have the bed, dear. I can easily sleep on the couch."

"Certainly not. I wouldn't dream of it."

They were making their way back to Mrs Rees's room. She always changed for dinner and saw no reason why death should interfere. "I dressed when both my husbands died. Why not now?"

"Let me give you a hand, at least." The arthritis was bad tonight, Clarissa noticed. The mottled hands were shaking.

She eased the lace dinner gown over Mrs Rees's coiffure and found a shawl. The elderly face looked so drained she asked uncertainly, "Maybe I should ask Hugh to have a look at you? Or Dr Willoughby as he's the official doctor here."

"Not him." Edith Rees was adamant. "Your young man perhaps. He looks harmless enough. What I really need is a brandy."

"Oh, so do I!" The events of the past 24 hours were catching up with Clarissa.

There was a knock at the door. She opened it. Mr Pringle stood, hands clasped in an attitude of prayer.

"Good evening again, Miss Pritchett. So sorry to intrude . . ."

"Who is it?" Mrs Rees asked.

"The detective, Mr Pringle."

"Ask him to come in. He probably knows where they keep the spirits." Clarissa held open the door.

He went through the preliminaries with grave courtesy, then gave Mrs Rees one of his forms. He sat quietly while she read it through. "I am quite prepared to answer most of your questions, Mr Pringle. The answer to the last one, I will give you in confidence, not in writing."

Looking over her shoulder to remind herself what this was, Clarissa was startled. "Edith, surely you never knew Von Tenke?"

"Not me, dear, no. George did. My second husband," she explained. Mr Pringle inclined his head and leaned forward to catch the rest of it.

"George and Valter Von Tenke committed sodomy together. Or do I mean buggery? I've never been quite sure what the difference was and it's difficult to find out. Do you know?"

"Edith!!"

G. D. H. Pringle made no immediate reply. Looking at him, Clarissa decided that he, too, needed a restorative. He moistened his lips. "I think . . ." he ventured, "under the circumstances the er, precise technical difference is — immaterial?"

"All the same, I would like to know."

"A — dictionary?" he asked hopefully.

She shook her head. "I've looked."

"Did he recognize you, Edith? Valter Von Tenke? You never said."

"No, he didn't. Why should he? We never met. That side of George's life happened in London, never at the Manor. I

99

refused to allow it and I'm sure Jonty never talked about it. It was a black secret in our lives . . . No, Von Tenke's photograph was one of those in George's dressing room. Along with others of course, all much younger than George. . . they always were. I wasn't sure at first, then yesterday, as he walked along the corridor towards me, I was sure. D'you remember? When you saw me in the Solarium, you said I wasn't looking well. . . ?"

"Yes."

"Well, it was a nasty shock. Once a sodomite, always a sodomite, or so I was told. Perhaps Mr Pringle knows if that's true also?"

If he did, Mr Pringle intended keeping the knowledge to himself.

"Did your son, did Mr Powers recognize Mr Von Tenke?"

"No. He kept well away from my second husband. He boasted about his money of course, Jonty would — 'my stepfather at the Manor' — that kind of thing, but I made sure they met as little as possible. He certainly kept out of George's rooms."

"Quite so." Mr Pringle consulted his notes. "Returning, if I may, to the events of last night and early this morning, might I ask you to describe what you did after Miss Pritchett and Dr Godfrey left the dining room . . . I do not wish to impute anything," he said to Clarissa, helplessly. "It is simply a useful starting point from which to ask people to recollect their movements."

"It was a starting point for Clarissa too, wasn't it dear?" Mrs Rees was beginning to recover.

"I'm going to look for that brandy." Clarissa moved to the door.

"Are you really?" There was no mistaking the appeal in Mr Pringle's voice. Clarissa wasn't entirely heartless.

"Don't worry. If I find any, I'll bring back the bottle."

Once she'd left, Mr Pringle felt extremely vulnerable. He appeared to find the area of carpet in front of him extremely interesting, and stared at it, wondering what he dare ask next. Mrs Rees brooded about her dead. The excitement her revelations had caused fast dissipated. Now she remembered only the beastliness.

"George married me when I was a young widow with a child. I'd led a very sheltered life, even when married to Harold. George knew this. I think he thought he could . . . mould me. Persuade me to behave disgracefully. When I refused, he sought solace elsewhere. He needed me in other ways . . . as a respectable front. . . against unpleasantness. He had plenty of money. It is easier to indulge oneself — and avoid trouble — if one has plenty of money. He was wicked . . . evil with both men and women . . . and violent. He and Valter had that in common in the end, both of them had such bitter deaths."

"Indeed?"

"George killed himself. He didn't mean to but that is how it turned out because I was unable to fetch help in time."

Mr Pringle was listening with a great deal of attention.

"He'd had too much to drink — arrived home drunk. He'd been quarrelling with someone. He kept telephoning them, shouting. . . the person still refused to see him. Quite a few were doing so by that time, George's appetites had become quite gross. . ."

The elderly well-bred voice was quiet and factual. It shocked Mr Pringle. "How very distressing."

"Yes . . . anyway, George shut himself in his car with the engine running and a tube from the exhaust pipe. He intended, I believe, simply to make a fuss. Prove to his latest victim how desperate he was for him — or her. I couldn't get the car door open. The police discovered afterwards it was locked. Nor did I think to break a window. Our telephone wasn't working properly, so I walked round to a neighbour. Quite a delay, with my hip. George was dead by the time help arrived."

"Did he leave a note?" Mr Pringle asked gently.

She didn't look at him. "If he did the police never found it."

"Your first husband, Harold. How did he die?"

She still didn't look at him. "He had a weak heart," she said shortly. She had been considering handing over her discovery to Mr Pringle but decided against it. His sudden question about

Harold had unnerved her. She pulled her shawl round her shoulders. "Do you think you could put more logs on the fire? The nights are drawing in."

As he built up a blaze, Mr Pringle wondered if that was the answer to his question, or not.

As darkness spread over the moor, the police brought in arc lights so that the frogmen could continue. Guests watched the detritus of centuries brought to the surface. No one, not even Mrs Arburthnot, knew what they were searching for. Looking at the spoils, Hugh wondered if any other nation concealed so many bicycle frames in stagnant stretches of water. He felt cold. So did many others. Excitement had faded and was replaced by an insidious feeling: fear. Even the uplift produced by the wine failed to dispel it. It sidled up behind, tapping unexpectedly on nervous shoulders, making hearts jolt — because one of them was a killer.

Of course, they knew it must be Dr Godfrey despite his protestations because Mr Powers had been so insistent. But after the scene in the library Miss Fawcett wondered aloud whether it might have been Miss Kelly instead? The police were still searching for her. But supposing it was neither of them? There was no apparent reason why it should have been.

In the topmost room of the tower, the Solar, Dr Willoughby and the Colonel stood drinking gin. The tower contained the Willoughbys' private rooms and this was the most splendid of all. The two men were apart, the doctor staring out of a window but he wasn't enjoying the view: he was agitated. This was the first occasion he'd been alone with his brother since he'd returned. He learned the full horror of the killing, now he couldn't bring himself to ask the one question that really mattered. He was momentarily distracted by a toy car, crawling up the drive far below, its blue light flashing. He waited until this had been switched off. "You don't think Miss Kelly had some kind of grudge? Something connected with your time in Northern Ireland?" It was an oblique approach but the doctor was nervous. He didn't want to be more specific.

"That was years ago. Anyway, what kind of grudge?"

"Thought she might have had a relative, caught up in the Troubles."

The Colonel stared at him over the top of his glasses and Tom Willoughby said diffidently, "I was trying to think of a reason, why she came, why she's run away." The Colonel sniffed and refilled his glass. "She came because she'd got some kind of infection — you told me that — must have thought this place was some kind of bloody hospital. My opinion. . . should have been told to go straight back to Killemorragh. She's run away because she's clearly unbalanced."

"You don't think it's because. . . she's got some connection with Valter Von Tenke?"

"Don't be bloody stupid." And the Colonel stared at the activity round the police car below.

Tom Willoughby tried again. "Consuela overheard one of the officers say that Miss Kelly may know who the murderer is."

He'd caught his brother's attention now. "Why?"

"She was in the room next door. She's supposed to have heard something." The Colonel favoured him with a long stare and said coolly, "How can you be sure he was killed in his room? He was found in the Solarium." Tom Willoughby stammered in his anxiety, "Yes I know that. Gerard, you invited him and I don't want to know the reason why, your friends are your own concern. I never liked the man — but it wasn't you. . . You didn't kill him did you?"

It had happened so many times before in their lives, the younger man begging the elder for reassurance, to make everything right again. The Colonel's smile was cold. "You've been trying to ask me that ever since you arrived, haven't you Thomas?" Tom Willoughby didn't reply.

"Answer me!"

"Well, naturally I was concerned — "

"Concerned! You — concerned! All you and Consuela care about is the bloody business! How will this damage the Health Farm's reputation, that's all you talk about, isn't it? Now you come traipsing back up here with this — this snooper!"

The Colonel's rage was loud but it always had been. Tom Willoughby stood his ground, not because he felt brave but because he had to know. "You haven't answered my question," he said quietly. The answer was a long time coming. The voice would have sent a shiver through the ranks.

"I didn't strangle Valter Von Tenke and you can tell your snooper yourself because I'm not filling in any of this civil service rubbish!" The Colonel flung his recycled envelope on to the flames. Tom Willoughby was so relieved, he babbled, "I'm sorry, Gerard, but you seemed so unconcerned. After all a man has been killed, someone you yourself invited, and so far I haven't heard you utter one word of remorse which under the circumstances — "

This time the Colonel was incandescent with anger, "Be quiet! One more word, Thomas, and you'll be sorry for it! Valter's death has nothing to do with you, Consuela, anybody — he's dead! All this," his wave encompassed the activity below, "none of it will bring him back. Let those stupid police poke and pry and then get the hell out of my home."

Tom Willoughby daren't leave the subject now. "The last officer was stupid, I grant you. The next may not be. It looks as if he's just arrived."

"I did not strangle Valter."

"They will still want to question you."

The Colonel sneered. Tom Willoughby persisted, "I've told Pringle to let me know anything he discovers but I can't silence him. He'll consider it his duty to pass on anything relevant to the police."

"Then you've brought it all on yourselves, you and Consuela, bringing him up here. If he opens Pandora's box, you've only yourselves to blame."

In the big old-fashioned kitchen, staff were filling in Mr Pringle's forms. Consuela managed to imply that since the police were obviously untrustworthy, their true allegiance lay here. They listened, docile, obedient. She left and now all was concentration.

"What does 'Siblings' mean?"

"In this instance, whether you have any brothers or sisters."
Mr Pringle was surrounded by delicious smells. Dare he ask for
a cup of tea? At noon, something brown and strange in an
earthenware dish had been sent in to him. Until today his idea
of vegetarian food had been a Ploughman's lunch. He decided
not to risk it.

"You all right, Wilf?" Millicent asked abruptly.

Mr Pringle looked at the masseur. Under the overhead light,
his pallor was obvious.

"Do you not feel well?"

"It's his mother," Millicent explained, "they won't let us
leave the castle at the moment and she depends on him, doesn't
she Wilf? It's her routine."

"She knows when to expect me," Wilfred said dully.

"That's what I mean. Why it happened. She's eighty-six,"
Millicent continued as though this made everything clear.

"They oughtn't to let them carry on at that age, did they?"

If he was being appealed to Mr Pringle turned a deaf ear. It
was precisely this sentiment that had led to his first murder
investigation. "What happened?" he asked.

"The police had to send someone else round because I
couldn't go."

"But they were too late for her routine," Millicent burst in.
"That's why Wilf's so upset. I mean, once a day is bad enough
but to have to clean her up twice. . ."

Wilfred shifted slightly. "She can't get out of bed, you see,
can't attend to herself. I do everything for her — I don't mind
— but she relies on me. And nobody told her I wasn't coming.
They didn't phone. Then they got there too late. She'd been
lying in her own filth all day."

"Now they've put her in the Geriatric," Millicent added,
pursing her mouth with disapproval.

There was silence. Wilfred sat, looking at nothing,
massaging the fingers of his hands automatically, loosening
and rubbing each joint. His white vest and trousers were

immanculate, as was the coat hung on the back of his chair. Did he never get dirty, Mr Pringle wondered. Even his skin had a cleanliness about it that made the black body hairs an anachronism. Suddenly the man began to cry. Jessie reached out a hand and patted him clumsily. He shook her off as if he couldn't bear being touched, "I always promised I'd look after her. Promised her she wouldn't end up in there!"

"Does Madam know?" Millicent asked.

"No. I haven't been able to see her to tell her."

"She'll know what to do for the best."

As if on cue, Consuela walked back in, switching on more lights. Mr Pringle was aware of an instant release of tension. They looked towards her confidently while Millicent once more prompted Wilfred through his tale. Mr Pringle listened carefully. None of Consuela's suggestions were remarkable, everything they could have worked out for themselves had they wanted to, it was simply that she expressed them, therefore these were the actions Wilfred must take. Mr Pringle didn't himself understand the urge to tug the forelock, to be told what to do, but he recognized it in others. These people needed their lodestar. Now they were satisfied. And what did they do in return? Protect the Willoughbys? He thought it quite likely they would lay down their lives for them.

To Mr Pringle, it was disturbing. Surely all of them had a private existence other than serving the family? Wilfred's he now knew about but what of the others? The only one amongst them with a bit of spirit was Mrs Burg. He gathered up his forms. Consuela had issued orders concerning the guests and he could see how anxious the little group was to carry them out. He was an intruder into their tight, fragile community. They wanted him gone. He tried squeezing one more morsel of information out of them. "When did the Colonel and Mrs Willoughby first meet?" No one answered at first, then Jessie said, "She'd already met him when you knew her, hadn't she Millie?"

Junoesque shoulders shrugged, Millicent frowned, "I believe she had, yes . . ."

They sat, waiting for Wilfred to speak. "Out East," he said eventually. Mr Pringle would dearly have loved to ask more questions but he could see it was pointless. He withdrew. Would the police have better luck? He doubted it. Loyalty was paramount below stairs at Aquitaine. They had rehearsed their replies and knew how far they were prepared to go with information. All the same, he would like to bet that that little group knew every single detail about the Willoughbys from the day they were born.

By a lamp in the corridor he paused to examine three of the forms. Jessie, Wilfred and Millicent all came from villages in the area; Wilfred and Millicent had spent last night at the castle. The reason in Millicent's case was clear. She had no other address than the castle. He found that odd. Surely such a capable woman needed independence. He read details of her background: father — 'former farm labourer', so who had paid for her training? She was a divorcee. Perhaps an alimony payment had made it possible. Her parentage was reflected in her shoulders and big strong hands.

Wilfred's answers were interesting. 'Mother: Ivy Bessie Wilson, maiden name Green.' In the space for his father's details Wilfred had written 'died 1953'. Odd. Most would have volunteered more than that. Under 'Siblings?' was an even bleaker phrase: 'one sister sent for adoption'. Mr Pringle looked again at the dates of death and birth, and thought he understood.

Chapter Four

DETECTIVE INSPECTOR KEATLEY arrived before dinner. Looking down from the Solar, the Colonel had said as he got out of the car, "Looks like a small fella this time. Wonder what his weakness is?"

There was an uneasy truce between them. Tom Willoughby was convinced his brother knew more than he'd admitted so far — but Gerard refused to speak further. The doctor's only consolation was that his brother would behave in the same manner with the police. He would have to wait until Pringle delivered his report and then decide what to do next. With any luck it would be before the police made any discoveries. With a great deal of luck, Gerard might not be implicated.

"Wonder if this one really will find out. . ." he said, but Gerard didn't respond. "What I'm most worried about is an open verdict — person or persons unknown — that will cause cancellations. Perhaps we should begin arranging some PR? Consuela and I were thinking of inviting some of the expensive magazines for a free weekend."

The Colonel wasn't interested. As far as he was concerned, God would provide and he, Gerard Mayhew Willoughby, need not lift a finger to help him. He read the second lesson occasionally and put a large banknote ostentatiously in the Easter and Christmas collections — what more could the deity expect? The thought — though true — that the Health Farm profits enabled him to go on living at Aquitaine — was disagreeable, so he ignored it. The unpleasantness this morning he regarded in much the same way, and thought it foolish to have involved a private detective. Somewhere behind the pig-headedness and stubborn refusal to accept facts was the knowledge that paying guests were necessary, which was why he agreed to 'press the flesh'. It also appealed to his vanity to patronize these strangers on Sunday nights in the library but by Tuesdays, he'd lost all curiosity and went his own way. Tonight was different. He stared at the dark moor. "Could be quite a frost. Nasty night to be out. That bloody Irishwoman could freeze to death, don't you think?"

Tom Willoughby closed his eyes. One body might be glossed over, two — never.

"Did you realize Consuela once knew Valter?"

"Pardon?" The doctor was alert now.

"Yes, met him when she was in Singapore. Before she met me. I never knew before, though. She mentioned it this afternoon."

"Dear me, dear me! I hope she didn't tell the police?"

"Course not. None of their business. Told her not to myself!"

"Very wise, Gerard."

Gin was turning the Colonel broody. "Think your chap will pull it off?"

"I honestly don't know," his brother replied nervously. They were on delicate ground he felt sure. "He beavers away. . . discreetly. Don't ask me how but his methods seem to work. Confidentially, he once stopped me making a complete fool of myself with a death certificate." He took a sideways glance at Gerard — he'd never uttered that to a soul before — but the Colonel was looking at his watch. On Tuesdays he was also excused boots in the dining room and partook of protein elsewhere.

"Grouse tonight," he announced cheerfully. "In my study so the beggars can't smell it. Drive 'em wild if they did. Here, your snooper isn't expecting to join us, is he?"

"Certainly not. He'll eat with the staff."

Useful though private detectives might be, their position in life was clear.

Mr Pringle feared he might have to forgo dinner altogether. He had to complete his examination of the rooms. He'd waited until the police had finished, and ruffled feathers were smooth again after the guests had been allowed to return and put their belongings to rights. Unlike the police, he didn't expect to find anything — he didn't know what they were looking for — but he wanted to build up a complete picture of each individual. He had announced his intention over punch in the library. No one had actually refused but Mrs Arburthnot began behaving coyly. For once Mr Pringle ignored the protest. He moved swiftly along the corridor, the pass-key in his hand.

Somewhere close by the constabulary were enjoying fish and chips. Saliva filled Mr Pringle's mouth, one of his old-fashioned sock suspenders chafed a varicose vein, but there was an art catalogue tucked in his attaché case that lured with a siren song. If he could complete this investigation by Friday and claim the bonus Dr Willoughby had promised, Lot 189 might be within reach. It was a small drawing, the beginnings of brush strokes delineating the central group of figures — men and women round a Northern market stall — the whole thing still pinned to a piece of blockboard with the provenance: 'Found among the Artist's personal effects.' How Mr Pringle yearned to possess it! In his mind's eye he could already see it on the wall above his desk. He unlocked a mahogany door.

The first things he saw were the brandy bottle and glasses. Miss Pritchett was obviously a resourceful young woman. Then he noticed the blankets and pillows piled on the couch and thought this sensible. Mrs Rees was a frightened old lady. Mr Pringle, too, was afraid. No intuitive flash told him why Von Tenke had been killed. The barbarism of the act sickened him, the apparent illogicality disturbed him. If there were no reason behind it, might not the killer strike again? Courage, he told himself, this sort of fear was based on ignorance. He must get at it, sort out the facts, elucidate. . . He thought again of Mrs Rees. Her fear was based on what she knew, he felt sure. He remembered her final question, "Do you think there will have to be another?"

"Another killing, you mean?"

Tired old eyes looked at him out of a face that suddenly crumpled. "I'm afraid I don't know," he'd said gently. "It would depend on why the first was — " he'd nearly said "necessary" but substituted "on why Mr Von Tenke was killed."

There was a pause before she'd asked, "I suppose all this has to continue? What you and the police are doing?"

"If we are to discover the identity of the murderer, certainly."

She had spoken incoherently then about it not being murder but an extermination of evil. Mr Pringle had expostulated. Surely every human being had a right to his or her natural span? When he saw how upset she was, he'd changed tack and began asking about Jonathan instead. She'd recovered a little when describing how much she disliked him, how insincere he was. Mr Pringle agreed, silently. His opinion of an industry prepared to tolerate such a poseur sank to new depths. As a tax man he was accustomed to television geniuses whose creative assaults on Schedule D beggared belief. He'd shut his ears to their wild outpourings when he'd unravelled their lies. Looking back, he was thankful he'd been spared Jonathan P. Powers in his districts.

Clarissa's room was sedate, all possessions neatly hidden away. Mr Pringle looked for some trace of identity but could find none. There were few clothes. Miss Pritchett travelled light. He could see no books and hesitated to pry. If a person took such pains with their privacy, Mr Pringle shrank from invading it. All the same, the word 'secretive' sprang to his mind as he closed and relocked the door.

Mrs Arburthnot's room was overflowing. Even to venture in was to invite disaster. Mr Pringle looked for a way through the obstacles. Shoes were strewn everywhere, the wardrobe door would not shut against the clothes and a brief glance into the bathroom made him quail. So many potions! And why leave an unrinsed razor like that? He sniffed fastidiously and examined the bottles. Most were marked 'Tester'. Back in the bedroom he saw magazines that lacked front pages. Had these been torn away because they had library stamps on them? He eased a couple of dresses from the wardrobe and took them to the window. It must not be supposed that Mr Pringle knew about fashion. Had he been asked afterwards what colour they were, it is doubtful whether he could have answered correctly, but he knew about line. He'd been taught the importance of it by his grandmother when helping with her treadle. He remembered her card in the front parlour window as if it were yesterday:

FORMER ASSISTANT TO
COURT DRESSMAKER.
Alterations a speciality.

She had shown him the difference between good and badly cut clothes, how to use his fingers to evaluate cloth. He used them now and decided the material was silk but worn very thin in places. There was an acrid body odour impregnated in it. The hem was inexpertly sewn up. Mr Pringle stood back and looked critically at the shape — surely ladies no longer wore such tight bodices? He opened one of the magazines and examined the Princess of Wales' chest. As he thought, covered in soft folds of material. Neat waists were 'in', too. He looked again inside the wardrobe, at some of the labels in the garments. Mrs Arburthnot's clothes were, he decided, second-hand and out of date. By having so many, perhaps she hoped to impress people. He remembered the proprietress of a 'Nearly New' establishment describing her clientele. "They're the nouveau poor dear, with ideas above their station. Easy meat. If you've got tired old stock, tell them a Duchess wore it and they'll grab it out of your hand."

He looked at the photographs. Groups of women smiled back at him from beside a tropical swimming pool. In the background, white-coated bearers waited, ready to pander to the Memsahibs' whims. Pampered useless women who'd been swept away as the Empire dwindled and, if Miss Brown were to be believed, Mrs Arburthnot longed to be thought one of them. At the bottom of the waste-paper basket was a mound of confetti. Fitting a few of the pieces together, Mr Pringle saw the sums. The lady had been calculating down to the last penny how much her bill at Aquitaine would be.

It all tallied with Miss Brown's description but why had Mrs

Arburthnot visited Valter Von Tenke in his room last night?

Miss Brown's shoes stood in a row covered in mud. She spent as much time out of doors as within, he judged. He noted the photograph of the grave. Wherever he stood in the room, he had an uninterrupted view of it. Why? Was Miss Brown afraid of what lay hidden beneath that mound of earth?

Hugh's clothes were everywhere. Mr Pringle shook his head. It baffled him just how untidy doctors could be. It was the same with their accounts. Hugh had bought a postcard, he saw. It lay face down and Mr Pringle read the words 'Dear Marion', that was all. He thought he understood why Dr Godfrey found it difficult to proceed.

He was about to unlock Jonathan's door when an official voice called out, "Just a minute". It was the sergeant who had been assisting Detective Inspector Robinson. Mr Pringle couldn't remember his name. "Yes, officer?"

"You're wanted. Downstairs. By the new boss."

There was an insolence about it as if by refusing to name him, the sergeant diminished the new man's authority. Mr Pringle was interested. D.I. Robinson's team had been close knit. He had heard them talking affectionately of 'old Robbie' — weaker men fawning round a bully, wanting to be part of his gang — the chosen ones. Now their leader had been taken away in disgrace. How far had his contagion spread? In his own Inspectorate there had been one or two, similarly tainted. It could infect not only the weak but those who believed themselves immune, in an unguarded moment.

Mr Pringle possessed no magic talisman against it. He simply believed that to take that which was not his, was wrong. What did it matter if those whom he assessed earned double his own salary? When he was offered a bribe, as he sometimes was, he always made the same reply: the would-be donor was breaking the law and the Commissioners would have to be informed. Incredulous laughter occasionally told him much that he would have rather not known about his colleagues.

He'd had a lonely existence after his wife died. Theirs had been a contented marriage, not that they'd made a fuss about it.

He'd stood by the hospital bed in silence, accepting tea and expressions of regret and got through the funeral as best he could. Then he went to the supermarket to buy half the quantities on their weekly shopping list. As he tried to remember which marmalade Renée always chose, Mr Pringle came to a decision. The aching void could have no adequate replacement, he'd never looked at anyone else since meeting Renée, he would learn, therefore, to endure loneliness. Fortunately Art provided a little consolation.

Six months after the funeral he began Life Classes. After a few weeks, when a 'flu epidemic was at its height, a harassed secretary told 'Beginners in Oils' that he'd managed to find a model — Mrs Bignell would oblige — but not an instructor. As the students assembled round the dais, several recognized that Mrs Bignell normally obliged behind the bar at 'The Bricklayers'. The senior student took charge. He asked her to take off her wrap and find a comfortable position. Mavis Bignell stripped and stretched out luxuriatingly on the model's throne. "I've never been nude in front of so many blokes before. . ." she had a rich, joyful laugh, "but it's great to take the weight off me feet!"

The younger men looked at her with distaste. They were accustomed to boyish, sexless anorexics whom they could view with clinical detachment. Here was flesh — masses of it. Mrs Bignell reminded them of their mothers — and mothers were not supposed to take off their clothes — but Mr Pringle thought of Rubens and his heart leapt. Soft arms lay across the ample stomach, vast thighs splayed in front of him and round, high breasts jutted enticingly. Her pubic triangle was on his eyeline, bright Titian gold strands reflecting the light. Mr Pringle picked up his new painting board and attacked it. This was no occasion for caution. Voluptuous creamy white piled up in layers as if he were trying to form the contours of the flesh itself. 'Venus Reclining' took shape under his feverish hand. There was no pause, he was swept along on a tide of erotic thoughts. Even during the tea-break he worked on, filling in the background with a classical olive grove.

The town-hall clock struck ten and the senior student told Mrs Bignell to relax. She put on her wrap and walked round the circle. Those who had only sketched with charcoal she dismissed as work-shy, those who had produced slim-looking bodies from memory were told they weren't using their eyes. Protests began. Models were not expected to comment but Mavis had discovered Mr Pringle. "He's got it right. Come over here and have a look, all of you."

Reluctantly they grouped behind her. Huge arms and legs bulged under the weight of their own paint, the vast body lay at an unlikely angle and the pubic triangle made them blink. Out of her moonlike face, Venus appeared to wink disconcertingly at them. Behind her, in the olive grove, a strange creature pranced eagerly. In the shocked silence a voice said, "It's awful!"

"No, it's not." Mrs Bignell was completely satisfied. "It's smashing. And it's finished." She turned to the exhausted creator. "It is finished, isn't it?" He nodded. "I knew it was. I could tell by the paint." She turned to the sniggering group, "You see — that's what you lot could do if you'd put your backs into it."

It was too much. They hastened away, packing wet palettes with reckless speed. Mrs Bignell waited until the last was out of earshot then nudged him. "What I think is so clever is the way you can see I fancy a bit." Mr Pringle blushed.

Later, much later, after a pleasant drink and a bit of supper, she asked, "Why d'you put a goat in it?"

"Oh — you mean the satyr!"

"What's a satyr?"

Mr Pringle explained.

"Is that why he's got a little willie? Is that where the goat ends and the man begins?"

Mr Pringle wished he'd studied their anatomy more closely but she didn't wait for an answer. Turning on her side she pointed to the wall opposite the bed. "I'm going to hang it up there. Okay?"

He'd switched to watercolours shortly afterwards. In a way, Mavis was sorry but she knew he was unlikely to better his masterpiece. She bought a nice frame at Boots and had the bedroom repapered creamy pink. Mr Pringle spent Tuesday evenings at 'The Bricklayers' and accompanied her home afterwards. The arrangement suited both of them. Once, perhaps out of a sense of guilt, he'd suggested matrimony. She waved the idea away. "You don't want that. Be honest dear, you don't — do you? Besides, I'm not prepared to give up me widow's pension. If you'd known Herbert, you'd understand. No, let's stay as we are. I like a bit of romance, okay?" And Mr Pringle was very, very grateful.

He thought of Mrs Bignell now as he walked along beside the large policeman. He would send her a postcard, one of those he'd seen on sale in Reception, quartered with four views: York Minster, Brontë parsonage, Whitby and Fylingdales Early Warning System. Across the whole, entwined with heather, was the message 'Good Neet fra' Yorkshire'. He was sure she would appreciate it.

Chapter Five

DETECTIVE INSPECTOR KEATLEY had worked in Lancashire and Yorkshire constabularies and possessed the rare distinction of being disliked by both. Normally he didn't care: on this occasion he was angry. He'd been dragged away from a case — handed over by one Chief to the other. Because of Robinson. What was nearly as bad, they'd sent him on his own, with no back up. No one with whom to share his thoughts, to chew over the case. Of course Robinson's lot were still there, waiting for him. But he wouldn't trust them — how could he?

It was a lousy assignment. He could picture the two Chiefs having a good laugh about it, once they'd got over the fact of Robinson. D.I. Keatley was a hard man, working class. Give him a body in a council flat, a mugging, he knew where he was, knew the people. How far to push, where to draw the line. If they were afraid, that was fine by him. Made them a lot easier to handle, which was what mattered. But this little lot . . . And he had to start by climbing out of the shit!

He had no illusions about Robinson. There'd been a smell in the air for ages. He'd heard the gossip. No smoke without that much fire. So here he was, on his own, in a bloody castle! He'd had to leave Davies to tie up the Video heist. Davies! Honest, but dim as a Toc-H lamp! Couldn't direct traffic on a wet Sunday in Pontefract, but that wouldn't stop him claiming the credit. Anger made the veins in his neck swell. D.I. Keatley had to remind himself that the rich had as much right to go on living as the poor.

He'd had himself driven to the mortuary first. That had sobered him up. The weal round Von Tenke's neck was nearly black where they'd cut away the strap. Fragments of leather were embedded in the skin. The eyes still stared and the fingers

117

of one hand were so tightly clenched they'd had to be forced open even though rigor was lessening. D.I. Keatley looked at the piece of metal they'd been clutching.

"Part of the fastening?"

"Yes. Look, I'll show you."

The doctor lifted it with pincers and placed it delicately against the helmet. It matched the other three buckles. The tiny cross-piece which had been snapped off gleamed brightly.

"Show me the pics again."

The attendant arranged them on the bench beneath the strip light. Four rows of three black and white twelve by nines of the corpse. D.I. Keatley concentrated on the side view of the head. The broken buckle showed up clearly. "So the poor bugger put up some sort of fight?" Like Hugh Godfrey, he was puzzled.

"Unfortunately he wasn't in a good position at the start." The doctor handed him the carbon copy of his preliminary notes.

"The top copy has already gone up to the castle. D'you want a photostat of this?"

"No, thanks." D.I. Keatley had reached the relevant paragraph.

"I see. Like that, was it?" He handed back the flimsy sheet.

"Can you wait for the full report till tomorrow? You've got the essentials there. It's late, the typist's gone home — "

"Yep. Tomorrow's fine." The inspector spoke absently, his thoughts elsewhere.

"You'd better call off the search."

"Mmm?"

"Robinson had a team of frogmen looking for that." The doctor indicated the piece of metal buckle. "I thought it much more likely it would turn up inside the castle, but you know Robbie. Call in frogmen — it'll look good on TV. As far as I know, they're still out there. Still searching."

D.I. Keatley looked at his watch and nearly boiled over again. At this hour! What about the bloody overtime! Stupid beggar — of all the pointless . . . ! He pulled on his coat, grabbed his set of the photographs and rushed outside, shouting his thanks and calling for the driver.

The police surgeon pulled off one rubber boot. "Right . . ." he said to the attendant, "put him away and start bagging up the bits for Forensic."

D.I. Keatley sat with the notes in front of him while he ate his supper. He speared the last greasy chip with his fork, thought better of it and shoved the plate to one side. There was a knock. The sergeant stood, filling the frame, but D.I. Keatley spoke first. "What I'd like now is a good strong cuppa with three sugars."

"I'm afraid you are doomed to disappointment. They only serve a herbal variety here, sweetened with honey." The disembodied voice spoke to him out of the darkness.

"Who the hell's that?"

"Mr Pringle, sir. The — private — detective." If the sergeant had sneered before, this time he went too far. D.I. Keatley spoke very sharply indeed. After today's cock-up the police were in no position to be rude, to anybody.

"Get me tea from our waggon, then. Good and hot, understand? And what about you, Mr . . . would you like a cup?" Mr Pringle came forward into the light. "That would be most kind. No sugar. I carry my own."

He would, thought the detective inspector, watching him fumble in a waistcoat pocket, and where on earth did anyone find him.

"Come in, come in. Sit yourself down. Right, Sergeant, at the double." Dismissed, snubbed, the big man slammed the door.

To be alone with the inspector was to be sniffed at by a bull terrier. Mr Pringle stood his ground and submitted. Unless he'd misjudged matters, D.I. Keatley had not found his second-in-command to his liking.

"Well, Mr . . . ?"

"Pringle."

"Pringle, yes. Are you going to tell me who did it, as in all the best fairy tales?"

"Unfortunately not yet. I hope, if possible, to have a clear idea by Friday."

"Friday? You're not giving yourself much of a chance, are you? Today's Tuesday."

"But the next group of guests are due on Saturday and the family want matters cleared up by then," he explained seriously, and added, "Dr Willoughby promised an enhanced payment should the case be resolved by then."

The voice was diffident but the inspector recalled the success rate of the Force. "Good luck," he said through clenched teeth. Mr Pringle sensed the interview wasn't going too well.

"I do this work to boost my pension. Normally I prefer to investigate fraud. There is very little pleasure in murder. Naturally, I only expect to receive expenses, should I fail. . ."

Detective Inspector Keatley tried to envisage police reaction to such terms, and shuddered. "If you do succeed, what will you do with the money? Go on a cruise?"

"Purchase a drawing, I hope."

The bull terrier was flummoxed. He tried to imagine wanting such an article himself. Those in his own home were good, he knew, his wife had paid over nine pounds for one of them — but to take on this job simply to buy one? He tried again.

"Well Mr Pringle, we both know why I'm here and why Robinson isn't — but I'm not going to waste time discussing that. . ." He paused to see if Mr Pringle wanted to dispute this but the man stayed silent.

"And we both know that you enjoy the confidence of, and have been employed by — the Willoughbys." Mr Pringle looked as if he wanted to clarify this but the Inspector held up a hand. "Hear me out. What I was going to say was, you've been brought in, as far as the guests are concerned, by them. By the family. And I'm quite sure those same people look on you as somebody different from one of us — right?"

Mr Pringle inclined his head.

"Now. . . I can assure you that Valter Von Tenke was killed by someone in Aquitaine Castle. The locks and bolts were all as they should be first thing this morning, we've checked, so. . . what I want to know is what you've found out. On your own. The confidential details that those sort of people. . ." His stubby finger pointed towards the door, "won't tell me."

Mr Pringle thought quickly. "I shall be most happy to co-operate," he replied, "if I may look forward to a reciprocal confidence in return — "

"Now just a minute — "

"That is not to suggest I wish for any favours, Detective Inspector Keatley." The bull terrier was glowering at him. "Merely that where any matter needs corroboration and you, with access to laboratory and research facilities, can supply it, might I hope that you will consider sharing such information with me? In confidence, of course?"

Privately, D.I. Keatley thought it would take longer than three days if everything was as longwinded as that. "I'm making no promises," he said curtly. Mr Pringle opened his old manila file.

"This is the situation as I understand it," he replied. There would be no concessions until he had proved himself. The inspector tilted back his chair and stared at the ceiling, jamming one foot in a drawer to balance himself.

Ten minutes later he was examining his own notes more closely. "That sequence of events tallies, apart from Mr J. P. Powers. D'you think Dr Godfrey can be relied on, in his estimates about the vomit?"

"Yes."

"So. . . the television gentleman was on the prowl too, last night. Not what he told my colleagues earlier, incidentally. Claimed he'd slept the whole night through. Now we know the approximate order of events, and we assume Maeve Kelly was the last person to admit hearing the deceased in his room — read that bit again. What Dr Godfrey told you she said."

Mr Pringle found the place. "She said something about he ought to be ashamed and that the Colonel — "

"Yes we know about the ruddy dog. 'Ashamed'. What d'you make of that?"

"What I have assumed all along, that Mr Von Tenke was overcome during copulation and the helmet — particularly the tight strap round the neck — was either to finish him off or conceal the method of killing."

The inspector was nodding. "Sexual activity confirmed in the p.m. report — Von Tenke was still alive when he went into the water, probably unconscious. But it needed a hefty woman to manage all that." He threw two or three photographs across the desk. Mr Pringle steeled himself. He'd asked to be admitted to the inner sanctum of police knowledge — here it was, in front of him. He forced himself to look at the photographs. D.I Keatley watched. Eventually Mr Pringle said, "Thank you Unfortunately I have not yet been able to establish whether the sexual act was normal intercourse or sodomy. Judging by the sword and belt, perhaps the latter is more likely?"

Across the desk, the inspector's eyes narrowed. "You what?"

"Mrs Rees. . ." Mr Pringle began and paused. The inspector's eyebrows shot up. "What about Mrs Rees? It says here she's seventy-two!"

"She recognized the deceased from one of her husband's photographs. He and Mr Von Tenke were lovers. Both men had, she believes, ambivalent attitudes to sex."

"AC,DC, you mean?"

"I believe I do, yes."

"Oh, that's charming! That's bloody marvellous — mind you. . ." The bubble of disgust burst as quickly as it had formed. "It makes more sense. I mean, look at the size of him. If it was a bloke that did it — "

"Or a man and a woman? Acting in concert?"

"Oh, bloody hell!" Unlike many of his profession, D.I. Keatley took no delight in what he defined as mucky cases. "Go on. Tell me the rest of it. What else was whispered in your shell-like ear?"

Mr Pringle told of his conversation with Miss Brown. At the finish, the inspector checked his own records again. "No," he said finally, "no mention of any note being found, and whatever D.I. Robinson may or may not have done, I'm sure he had that room taken apart."

"I'm sure he did," Mr Pringle soothed, "so may we assume that Mr Von Tenke had a further visitor after Mrs Arburthnot, or that she herself picked up the note?"

"I'm not assuming anything further." The inspector kicked the desk drawer shut. "I'm going to talk to them. Make up my own mind. Now, is that all you can tell me?"

"I think so." Mr Pringle made a pretence of looking at his file.

"You can let me know anything else that occurs to you, later. Come on. I gave instructions they were all to stay together in the dining-room. They've had enough time to stew. . ." He was tugging at the door because it appeared to be sticking. It burst open and there was a crash as the two mugs the sergeant was carrying hit the stone floor. He swore as hot wetness penetrated his trouser leg. "What kept you?" asked the inspector sarcastically, then, "leave it, leave it. . ." The man was picking up the pieces. "Get your book. We're going to start interviewing. . . Mr Pringle is going to introduce me to the gentry." Had he been accepted? Only while he remained of use, G. D. H. Pringle was sure.

During their brisk walk down the corridor, Mr Pringle volunteered cautiously, "Miss Kelly must be extremely hungry by now."

"We'll soon pick her up, don't you worry. . ." The inspector paused before adding, "She's part of a cell we've known about for some time — this is in confidence by the way. Financed by third-generation Irish Americans in Boston. Old men, dreaming dreams, with money to burn. No connection with Von Tenke that we know of, but we're checking."

"Dr Godfrey gave the impression she was very immature. And killing the dog had upset her."

"Maybe, maybe. . ." The inspector didn't speculate. He dealt in facts. As they approached the dining-room door he said sternly, "I want it clearly understood that you being with me is unofficial. If any of them object I shall have to throw you out. No argument. Also, under no circumstances will I allow you to interrupt. Right?"

"Certainly, Detective Inspector."

Inside, desultory chatter stopped immediately. Everyone tried to appear nonchalant; none succeeded. Mr Pringle went round, performing introductions courteously, the sergeant trailed behind the inspector. He loathed D.I. Keatley now. This was the final humiliation.

When he'd met everyone, Detective Inspector Keatley addressed the room. "Thank you for waiting so patiently. To those who have already been interviewed, I offer apologies but ask that you answer a few further questions. To the rest, I shall endeavour not to keep you waiting longer than necessary. Tonight, as it's late, I'd like to see Mrs Sheila Arburthnot, Dr Hugh Godfrey and Mr Jonathan P. Powers. That's all. Tomorrow, when inquiries are complete, you will all be permitted to use the telephone."

"I must protest."

"Yes, Mr Powers?"

"I insist I be allowed to contact a solicitor."

"A solicitor?" The inspector grinned savagely, "That's interesting. . . the last telephone number you gave the W.P.C. was for the *Sun* newspaper."

Jonathan opened his mouth, thought better of it and closed it again.

"Right, then. Mrs Arburthnot. . . ?" Sheila Arburthnot attempted skittishness.

"I fail to understand why I should be first?" she simpered. Jonathan sniggered unpleasantly.

"Perhaps they've found Von Tenke's will and he's left you all his money?" Sheila Arburthnot gasped and clung to her chair. Colour drained from her face leaving patchy make-up exposed. Hugh moved across, reaching for her wrist and asked if she felt ill. Clarissa said sharply, "Don't be so crude, Jonathan!" Mr Pringle raised his mild voice.

"The detective inspector will be talking to all of us, Mrs Arburthnot. It is simply that he would prefer to see you first, if you feel well enough."

Finding herself the centre of attention, she said coquettishly, "I've quite recovered, thank you Dr Godfrey. . . I cannot think what came over me. Perhaps it's my age. . . ?" There was an embarrassed silence because there was no possible reply. She rustled to her feet with a flourish of taffeta, "I'll lead the way, shall I? My suite is cosy and has all the facilities — "

"All interviews will take place in my office, madam."

Thwarted, angry, she flung herself back in her chair. "In that case I absolutely refuse. I've answered more than enough questions already — no one can force me to answer more. I know my rights." She stretched out an arm in mute appeal to Consuela. It was the inspector who answered her.

"Ladies and gentlemen, I am conducting a murder investigation. I can do so here or in the nearest police station but, as sure as God made little apples, that investigation will take place. Now, as to your rights. A constable will be present at all times and you will be asked to read any statement you may make before signing it, to ensure that it is correct. You may also decline to answer any of my questions, but that too will be noted. . ."

He let this threat hang over them a few seconds then continued, "If you wish to go to a police station instead of the temporary office here, you will be taken by police car, past any newsmen who may have gathered outside the gate, and you will have to make your own way back because I'm not wasting tax-payers' money providing a taxi service. Do I make myself clear?"

The silence was palpable. Hugh felt Clarissa's hand reach for his own and hold on to it, tightly. Nearby someone was breathing unsteadily. The inspector asked again, "Does anyone prefer that we go to the police station?" Silence. "Very well. I shall interview everyone who was present in Aquitaine Castle last night when Valter Von Tenke was so brutally murdered."

Mr Pringle watched faces turn red or white and could feel the tension build up. He found himself wishing he had been able to frighten some of his clients in taxation days but pushed the thought guiltily away. He neither liked nor disliked those whom he'd so far met. He found Dr Godfrey and Miss Pritchett quite pleasant and Mrs Willoughby beautiful to look at — how frightened she appeared to be now. Had she, like Mrs Rees, something to hide?

The inspector was saying, "If those whom I'm seeing tonight could keep themselves available, I'll wish the rest of you a very good night. Tomorrow. . ." He gave one of his lifted lip smiles, "you can all carry on with your cures."

And who, thought Mr Pringle, could resist an invitation like that?

The fire in the inspector's temporary office had been left switched on, the heat met them.

"Goodness," Mrs Arburthnot simpered, "I shan't need a wrap in here. I was considering asking your officer to bring one down, the squirrel one on a chair in my suite — "

"Sit down, madam."

And do please be quiet, Mr Pringle prayed inwardly, this man is dangerous.

She made a business of arranging her skirts. Mr Pringle again caught the acrid smell, a mixture of body odour and that scent Miss Brown had recognized. It was much stronger in the warm room.

"Well, Mrs Arburthnot . . . ?"

The inspector paused. It was all the encouragement she needed. She rushed heedlessly into her chosen role — a gushing society woman. "As I said before, I've absolutely no idea why you should pick on little me, unless you're being gallant, inspector. You wanted me to be the first to be put out of my misery, that was it, wasn't it?" She made what could only be described as a 'moue' and Mr Pringle wondered if there were a more inept word to use about D.I. Keatley. She favoured them now with a gracious smile. Sweat had caked the powder on her lip and jaw, it was a darker shade than her skin. "It's dear, dear Mrs Willoughby we should consider first," she told them, "one yearns to help, doesn't one? Too sensitive. And the Colonel — so instinctively generous. You know how it all started, don't you? The Colonel bumped into the wretched man in town, outside his club. Hadn't seen him for years and years! And Valter hinted so boldly about visiting Aquitaine — as the Colonel said, one couldn't refuse. Well, he wouldn't, would he.

Not a Willoughby. They're not the sort. Breeding. I'm afraid it always does show, doesn't it?" Deprecatingly, Mrs Arburthnot hitched her skirts a fraction too high and slid her legs seductively along the carpet.

Sitting behind, Mr Pringle could see her skinny thighs reflected in the shiny metal surround of the fire. Tired suspenders attached to what had once been lacy frippery but was now torn and dingy. As she crossed her calves and raised her knees even higher, he closed his eyes for fear of what else might be reflected but the inspector didn't look away. He was facing Mrs Arburthnot and smiled, encouraging her lemming-like indiscretion.

She paused only when sentiment about the Willoughbys ran dry. In the silence, did she experience her first moment of doubt? The inspector leaned forward, he didn't hurry. "Now madam. . . we're going to have to begin all over again, aren't we. . . and this time, let's have the truth." Slowly, deliberately, he tore what they could all see was her first statement in half, and dropped the pieces in the waste paper basket. Mr Pringle felt her shock. He listened as the inspector began to peel away the layers of lies, exposing social pretensions to shrivel in the heat of his scorn. He listened, too, to Mrs Arburthnot's tears coursing through the thick dark powder.

The inspector began by telling an untruth. He'd seen the photographs in the Plantagenet suite he told her, he knew about the life in Singapore. "But you weren't in those pictures, were you madam, because you weren't really part of that crowd? You wanted to be of course. What was your real position out there? Companion to some old lady? One of the servants?"

"No!" she cried out, "I may have been a nurse when I married Eric but I gave that up. And with his position, we were allowed to use the Services Club — "

"Allowed!"

Detective Inspector Keatley seized the word in his jaws and worried it almost to death. 'Fawned, crawled, begged,' he managed to imply them all in the way he kept repeating "Allowed. . . ! "

She was crying openly now. Mr Pringle was most uncomfortable. Why didn't the real questioning begin? But the inspector wasn't quite ready. This butterfly might still try and flutter out of his grasp. "When your husband hanged himself, did they still allow *you* to use the Services Club?"

"Who told you about Eric?"

Mr Pringle had registered the use of the word 'husband'? Was the inspector keeping bigamy as a dénouement, or didn't he trust Miss Brown's account?

"She told you, didn't she? Melody Brown? Never mind asking me about Eric, why not ask about her father dying like that — "

Melody, thought Mr Pringle? Oh dear, oh dear. . .

"Answer my question please, Mrs Arburthnot, and stick to the point. Were you allowed on your own in the Services Club? After your husband died?"

It poured out in a torrent, hoarse, unchecked. The bitchy community of service wives, making gossip while servants did the work, aping their husbands' ranks even in the seating round a pool. Mrs Arburthnot had never sat in a comfortable chair — oh, no — those were reserved for the Colonel's lady — but she had to belong to the club, not to do so meant becoming a social outcast, and she'd found out what that meant all right, after Eric's death. And belonging meant entertaining lavishly, inviting those same bitches even if she and Eric couldn't really manage it, joining in shopping expeditions in that Mammon's paradise where everything was so cheap you couldn't afford not to buy! As she described it, Mr Pringle felt the hot humid sun, saw the dyed coiffures, heard the ghosts of shrill Memsahibs clinging to their privileged little lives.

Eric started drinking, that's when everything went wrong — it wasn't her fault! Their fragile juggling act with money collapsed. Once he'd met Willie Brown, the rest was inevitable. Eric had been so weak.

"The truth, madam," the inspector persisted softly, "he needed the money to pay your debts, didn't he? You'd run up those enormous bills, far bigger than he could afford to pay. No doubt that's why he started drinking but not why he committed suicide, that's the real truth, isn't it?"

It was a dreadful accusation but oddly enough she didn't flinch. "Yes. . ." she answered flatly, "I suppose in a way it was my fault. . ." The inspector's next words were as hard as pebbles, "If you tell me any more lies, I shall know it." Sheila Arburthnot didn't look at him. The other two men held their breath. "Yes. . . I expect you will." Her voice was as monotonous but Mr Pringle strained to catch something else? Surely not — caution? Wasn't the butterfly pinned down, all resistance futile?

"Let's consider your situation, shall we madam? Your husband hanged himself because money he was expecting went missing — and he couldn't repay a loan. Miss Brown's father owned up, took his medicine. Your husband — took his own life. According to Miss Brown, you then disappeared. Now, why. . . ? They didn't realize at the club it was really your fault, did they? You no doubt convinced them — as you tried to do us — that your husband had a drinking problem . . . lots of sympathy from other wives, similarly afflicted, for a time anyway. No, my guess is it was money — or rather the lack of it — that was the reason you did a bunk, wasn't it?"

There was the slightest hesitancy before Sheila Arburthnot answered, "Yes . . ." The inspector didn't appear to notice.

"And I'd like to make a further guess — it was Valter Von Tenke who helped you do that bunk, wasn't it?" Mrs Arburthnot stared at him. The inspector leaned over the desk as he went in for the kill, "You're still the same person, aren't you, madam, still trying to be accepted, to be one of them?" He stabbed a finger in the air at the castle, the Willoughbys, the whole system that encouraged silly butterflies to flutter into the charmed circle of golden light.

When she spoke this time, Mrs Arburthnot's words came in an ever-increasing rush. Mr Pringle was disturbed. It didn't sound to him like an answer but a new idea that was evolving even as she described it. Yes, she'd recognized Valter, she'd reminded him of the old days and how he'd sometimes helped

Eric and herself over a rough patch — he could always afford it, he was an expert mining engineer, they could name their own price out east. . . "I went to his room last night, at his invitation, to talk over old times. I meant to ask for a loan, I admit, but I couldn't bring myself to. There was a coarseness about Valter. He'd changed so. As we talked it became more and more apparent. In the end, I simply excused myself and left." She gave the inspector a ravaged, confident smile.

"Was Von Tenke alive when you left?" The inspector was baffled, his question half-hearted. A moment ago, he'd had her, he knew. Now she was slipping away and he couldn't fathom why. A piece of paper slid into his hand. Mr Pringle had moved so stealthily the inspector had hardly been aware of it. Mrs Arburthnot was back to her gushing self, emphasizing how very much alive Valter had been, how difficult to get away. Her voice quavered a little as she saw him read the note. When he looked up at her, she stopped altogether. Detective Inspector Keatley's manner was now very cool indeed.

"Returning for a moment to that missing cheque all those years ago, you had it, didn't you madam? You kept silent while Miss Brown's father was punished and your husband, Eric, hanged himself? In the end you used it as barter, to extricate yourself. That's the real . truth, isn't it?" Sheila Arburthnot didn't need to speak: her face was grey. "You can't prove it," she whispered eventually.

"Valter Von Tenke guessed, though, didn't he? And that was the real reason you went to his room last night. Blackmail. . . !" The inspector's voice rose in triumph. "He'd threatened to tell the Willoughbys about you, hadn't he? Threatened to tell them the real reason for Eric's death — and by the way, madam, did Eric kill himself because of the shame of your debts, or because he, too, found out that you had the cheque, and couldn't bear that burden either? Your 'husband'. . ." he went on sarcastically, "the poor bastard had married you bigamously — he could have simply walked out. You'd have had no redress. . ."

"She told you that too, did she . . . Melody Brown?" No one answered. Instead, the Inspector stood and towered over her,

"Come on. You went to Valter Von Tenke's room because he knew what had happened all those years ago."

"I didn't steal the cheque . . . it was a gift."

"Oh, no. Valter Von Tenke didn't make gifts — he wasn't the type — wasn't a gentleman," the inspector sneered, "surely you recognized that? Breeding always shows, doesn't it?" He wasn't going to let her get away a second time. He bent down so that his lips were inches from her face, "I want to know exactly what happened. . ."

"I'd never expected to see him again . . . especially here. He demanded repayment. . . " Her voice was colourless. Was this finally the truth?

"I told him I couldn't possibly — I hadn't got the money. . . He threatened to tell the Willoughbys." She hesitated over saying that as if it was still too extraordinary a threat. She went on. "He had another suggestion. . . instead of repaying the money. . . to wipe out the debt. . ." In the pause that followed, Mr Pringle suddenly felt his stomach turn over. He'd guessed what the suggestion had been. So had the inspector.

"And that excited you, didn't it?" he hissed, pressing her. "Dr Godfrey and Miss Pritchett were flaunting themselves so why shouldn't you? Everyone does it nowadays, nobody minds. Liberation, that's what women call it when they sleep with anyone they fancy — and nobody'd fancied you, had they, for years and years. . . ?" It was cruel but the butterfly had nearly escaped. "A few nights, was that it? Not much for such an outstanding debt." The inspector went in for the kill, clenching his hands so they wouldn't betray him. "Only it wasn't quite like that, was it?" Silence. "Come on. Let's have the rest."

Outrage burned inside Mr Pringle. He'd been responsible but did they have to shame this silly stupid woman? Then, just as suddenly he thought of a man, a rope pulled tightly round his neck, squeezing the life out of him all those years ago.

"I was a bit nervous. . ." Sheila Arburthnot attempted to laugh. The men stared at her. "After the exercise class I should've realized. . . but I thought he would be different. . . and it had been a long time since. . ." her face implored but they

131

were impervious.

"Go on."

"He made it sound like quite the normal thing, until I got there." Her ghastly laugh wobbled into tears, "He made me undress, that was all he wanted." Remembering it made her shiver, her body bent in agony as she forced herself to describe the shame. "It was the most degrading. . . He sat — watching, saying things. He made me go on until I was naked. I had to stand in front of him — he humiliated me. In the end, I was sick. He laughed! He stood watching me being sick, and laughed. When I came out of the bathroom he said I could go. He was — evil!"

The inspector waited a fraction before he asked, "Is that why you killed him?" Mrs Arburthnot lifted her head and stared at him in surprise. When she spoke, her voice was back to normal, "Oh, no, I didn't kill him. What on earth makes you think that?"

Sheer relief threatened to overwhelm Mr Pringle. Surely now they'd heard the truth? He caught sight of the inspector's face and contained himself. D.I. Keatley looked so frustrated he thought he would explode. "I'm going to ask you one more time, madam. Did you kill Valter Von Tenke?"

"Certainly not."

Mr Pringle wanted to hug the awful wreck and tell her it didn't matter. Nothing mattered any more. Instead he sat completely still, not making a sound. Slowly, very slowly, it dawned on Sheila Arburthnot that everything had changed.

"Is that all?"

Detective Inspector Keatley didn't reply.

"I asked whether that was all?" The chrysalis was hardening now. Inside another life cycle was beginning. "Can I go?"

"I shall require you to sign a statement once it's been typed out."

"Provided it is accurate, I shall have no objection." She stood, making no attempt to smooth her skirts or wipe her face, but for the first time, Mrs Arburthnot had dignity. Mr Pringle moved instinctively to open the door.

"Just one more question, madam. What happened after

you'd been sick?"

"I told you — I went back to my own room." Her lip trembled as she remembered the obscenities that had followed her into the corridor.

"Were you naked?"

"I'd taken my clothes outside. I began to dress but I had to move. I heard a door being unlocked."

"Whose?"

"Mr Powers'. His room is next to Mr Von Tenke's. It sounded as if he was coming out so I hid by the fire escape in the corner."

Mr Pringle had a vision of her pulling on clothes over cold, clammy skin, terrified of discovery.

"Where did Mr Powers go?"

"I've no idea," she answered. "You'll have to ask him yourself."

"Did he go towards Mr Von Tenke's room or in the other direction?"

"Oh, he went the other way. I saw that much."

"And you went back to your room?"

"To my suite, yes."

"And spent the rest of the night alone?" This time the question was mechanical, he'd gone as far as he could, he was simply tying up loose ends.

"Of course I spent it on my own! How dare you imply — " But it was no use protesting, not after what they'd heard. Mr Pringle opened the door quickly, anxious to put an end to it.

As she walked past, Sheila Arburthnot said angrily, "I shall complain about your behaviour. I shall inform Mrs Willoughby I was subjected to — harassment." Mr Pringle bowed his head. The blame for what had happened was all to be his, obviously. So be it. He closed the door behind her. She would tell the others, he would be alienated now. One of 'them', the police.

"Cock-teaser." The inspector yawned and stretched. "Nothing like a vicious old queen for making a woman strip. Nazis used that technique on French women sometimes. . .worked better than torture." Mr Pringle didn't speak. He still felt shaken by the interview.

"Strong hands, did you notice? And admitted she'd been a nurse. All the same. . . "

"You don't think she was responsible?" asked Mr Pringle. The inspector didn't look up. He scribbled absently on his pad.

"Prefer to draw my own conclusions. Thought I'd made it clear — no interruptions, no notes, nothing."

"But. . ." Mr Pringle was astonished. Hadn't his note been relevant, been the turning point of the interrogation?

"I think it would be better if you worked independently from now on — right?" The sergeant smirked. Mr Pringle bowed his head for a second time, still without speaking.

"One more thing. As it's late, I don't think I'll bother with anything else tonight. Get that lot typed up, Sergeant, she can sign it tomorrow — 'Poor Eric was so weak'," he quoted, "The poor sod was doomed from the day he met the bitch."

Still stunned by his dismissal, Mr Pringle moved towards the door. There was no point in waiting. Had he caused the inspector loss of face by passing him that sheet of paper? He didn't know. The familiar voice broke through his thoughts, "Pringle, you might tell Powers and Godfrey, tomorrow morning will do. About eight-thirty. I need a good night's kip."

He'd been demoted to messenger boy. Mr Pringle's cup of bitterness overflowed. "Anything else?" he asked mildly. The inspector shifted a little in his chair. "No, I don't think so, thanks. We can manage."

That, Mr Pringle devoutly hoped, would not prove to be the case.

Nursing his hurt pride he wandered about aimlessly. He'd only been trying to help, on impulse. Seeing uniformed men and women busy in pursuit of the assassin made Mr Pringle even more determined: he would succeed. He gazed out of a window at the brightly lit caravan in the car park. The words INCIDENT ROOM were painted on the side. Inside he could see an officer typing. A phone rang, the ghost of the sound reaching him

134

across the moat. He watched as the constable picked up the receiver and adjusted switches on the large computer behind him.

"Looks impressive, doesn't it?" The voice was so close, the question so unexpected, Mr Pringle had to steady himself against the windowsill. He hadn't seen the W.P.C. in the dimly lit embrasure. It was the same girl who'd been operating the switchboard earlier. She, too, was looking at the caravan. "I can't wait to get my hands on it," she said enviously. Was she referring to the constable? Mr Pringle thought not but proceeded cautiously. "The — computer?" he asked.

"Yes. Bet you haven't seen one like that before?"

Mr Pringle readily agreed that he hadn't.

"D'you know how much it cost? Have a guess?"

He shrugged helplessly. Calculators had been the latest invention during his pre-retirement year. One per district, they were mounted on small wheeled tables, the theory being that they could then be moved to where they were most needed. To the end, Mr Pringle had never managed to qualify. He'd finished as he'd begun, with a slide-rule. "I've no idea," he admitted, "but it looks pretty sizeable."

"Two hundred and sixty-three thousand." She paused long enough for him to be impressed before adding, "But it doesn't work yet."

"Good gracious me, why not?"

"Came without the interface unit, didn't it. You'd think at that price it'd be included, but it wasn't."

Mr Pringle remembered he was a rate-payer. "You certainly would."

"Not any old interface will do, either," she confided, "it's got to be the one specially designed to fit — but that will give it two hundred and fifty thousand RAM!" The possibility left her breathless. Mr Pringle was sad that he couldn't share her enthusiasm. "What is it capable of doing at present?"

"Bugger all." She looked at the white elephant with a mixture of pride and disgust. "In there. . ." she pointed to the caravan, "we've got one copy of the handbook — translated from the

135

Japanese — and we're all supposed to make do with that until the new budget's been approved. So, P.C. Harrison uses it to work out his alimony payments and P.C. Duncan leaves rude messages on the screen which are supposed to make W.P.C.s blush. He's a sexist pig and he can't even spell."

Mr Pringle stood for a moment in silent sympathy before asking what marvels could be expected when the missing unit was available. "The interface? Oh well, the sky's the limit when we've got that. I mean, if we know the villain we're looking for is left-handed and has one blue eye — an operator will be able to punch up the names of all known left-handed, blue-eyed suspects within *three* seconds!" G. D. H. Pringle decided that the wheel had advanced mankind further. He ventured a little joke. "Perhaps you and your lady colleagues should buy the constable a dictionary." Her incredulity stopped short as she realized how old he was. "P.C. Duncan doesn't know any dictionary words," she said pityingly, "he uses the other sort."

Mr Pringle found privacy in a campaign chair on the first floor. He needed to disentangle his thoughts. Wilfred was moving in and out of the various bedrooms, delivering night-time Thermoses. He nodded to him as he went past. One or two things still weren't clear. Mr Pringle went through the various accounts of last night. He thought he now understood why Mrs Arburthnot had made no mention of Miss Brown's note: she presumably wasn't in Von Tenke's room when it was pushed under the door. Wasn't the reason Miss Brown was so aware of the 'niffy' perfume because the other woman was close by? Had Mrs Arburthnot been hiding or had she fled by then, leaving only the imprint of herself in the air? No matter. The note had been delivered and no one so far admitted knowledge of it.

And what did it contain? Mrs Arburthnot's wild cry — 'ask about her father dying like that' rang in his ears. Like what? Miss Brown was certainly haunted by that death, otherwise why carry the memory of the grave with her — and those casual references of hers to trust money. Had Valter discovered something about Miss Brown? As a blackmailer, he'd surely take advantage if he could? Mr Pringle sighed, remembering her muscular shoulders. She had the strength, but was it likely that any man would be seduced by Melody Brown?

Valter Von Tenke had been overcome at his most defenceless. How long did it take? How much pressure on carotid arteries before a healthy man succumbed and how long would he remain in that state? Mr Pringle needed to know. He remembered he had to deliver messages; one was for Dr Godfrey.

In room number one the fire had long since burnt to ash. Flames flickered occasionally as if anxious to prove they were still alive. Mrs Rees lay back against her pillows, clutching her handbag. Her eyes were closed but she was awake. The others sat round the fire. The room door was open as others were, up and down the corridor. No one wanted to be the first to shut himself away in the dark, to surrender to fear and to sleep.

Hugh realized he'd had too much brandy; he couldn't work out why this had happened. It was coursing through him, stinging him to life, infusing him with alternate desire and melancholy. He remembered the first couple of drinks when they'd got back to the room, then because Clarissa was such a marvellous person, he'd had a few more. He'd found himself thinking of Marion — which was terrible — so he'd had another one or two to forget her, but he couldn't. He was indignant with himself and with her for spoiling his mood. He wanted to think only of Clarissa. He looked fondly at her now as she walked across and stared at him. He reached for her hand but it was further away than he supposed, so he smiled at her instead.

"You're stoated," she said wearily, disgusted that he should exhibit his weakness in front of Jonathan and Mrs Rees. "You can't possibly talk to the police in that state."

The police? Why on earth should he want to talk to them?

"Chance would be a fine thing!" Jonathan said bitterly. "Look at the time, for Chrissake."

There was a polite cough from the doorway. "May I came in?" asked Mr Pringle.

137

"The very man." Jonathan equated him with law and order. "When am I to be interviewed? I've been waiting around like some fifth rate criminal — "

"In the morning, Mr Powers. You may retire now, if you wish. Detective Inspector Keatley asked me to tell both of you. . ." He looked at Hugh, ". . . that as the hour is late he has deferred further interviewing until eight-thirty tomorrow morning."

Jonathan exploded. Clarissa shook her head over Hugh.

"Thank goodness for that but I doubt whether he's understood."

"Oh dear. Is he, er. . . indisposed?"

"He's bloody drunk," said Jonathan contemptuously.

"Ah. . . I had hoped — a few questions of my own."

"Try him in the morning," Clarissa advised. "but not too early. Now, can the two of you get him back to his room?"

"Why should I help!" Jonathan was determined to lose his temper over something. "If the fool can't hold his liquor, why on earth — " There was another knock at the door. "Oh what is it this time?" Wilfred stood, carrying a small tray.

"Mrs Rees's drink, sir."

"Come in, come in."

He walked in soundlessly, put down the tray and exchanged a full ashtray for an empty one. Mrs Rees watched.

"Thank you," she said. "Would you put the fireguard in position please?"

"Certainly, madam."

There wasn't much likelihood of an accident, thought Mr Pringle, hardly a spark remained alight. Mrs Rees was speaking to him.

"Have the police discovered all they need?"

"I doubt it. I'm afraid they may be here for some days yet."

"If they cannot solve matters, when will they go away?"

"I think they may well succeed."

She stared at him. "A pity," and she closed her eyes again. Mr Pringle waited but she said nothing more.

In the end three of them helped Hugh upstairs. Mr Pringle

138

and Wilfred each took an arm, Jonathan supervised. It was a slow progress. Once inside number eight, Wilfred took charge, stripping Hugh of his clothes, putting on his pyjamas. Mr Pringle took the opportunity for a few words with Jonathan. "The police are aware that you were not in your room the entire time last night," he murmured, "so may I advise that you be. . ." He hesitated over 'honest', ". . . more straightforward tomorrow." Jonathan began to bluster. "There are witnesses," Mr Pringle insisted.

"Oh, very well. . . all this fuss. . . I was starving, you know, I had to find something to eat."

Mr Pringle turned to Wilfred. If Hugh was inebriated, at least there was one other source. "D'you think Dr Willoughby is still awake? And could be prevailed upon for a few minutes' conversation?"

"I think so, sir. He never retires early when he's here."

The batman's pallor had increased. Mr Pringle saw this with concern. "I hope the situation regarding your mother," he began, then paused. How could there be an improvement? Hadn't Millicent told him she'd been taken to the Geriatric?

"I'm to be allowed to go and see her tomorrow."

"Good, good. . ."

"Tomorrow. . . ?" Jonathan held open the door with a theatrical sigh. "Shall any of us live to see it? Well, if there's nothing more I can do here . . . ?" He wandered off down the corridor.

In his temporary office, D.I. Keatley wasn't having much luck. After Mr Pringle's lapse, he'd decided to rely on the sergeant. He was as hurt by Mr Pringle's intervention as that gentleman had been by his dismissal. He didn't mind assistance, D.I. Keatley told himself, provided it came from the correct quarter — and that was from a trained member of the Force. Now he was stuck with one. He'd given the sergeant sole responsibility for finding Maeve Kelly.

The man stood in front of him now, big, smug, God's gift in any pub brawl or for breaking up Peace demonstrations, but

D.I. Keatley had asked him to track down an Irish woman.

"It's okay, sir. We've got her cornered."

"Where? Downstairs?"

"No, not here in the castle. But it's all right, we know where she is. Roughly."

The inspector's eyes narrowed. "What d'you mean — 'roughly'?"

"She's somewhere near Pickering, we're sure of that."

"Sergeant, my patience is limited — "

"She held up a fish and chip shop."

"She did what!!"

"My theory is — she was hungry."

"Sod your theories!" The inspector still couldn't credit it. "Why didn't she buy them like anyone else?"

"She hadn't got any money. She offered a credit card but they don't accept them at the Chippy."

"Okay. I've got the picture. Then what?"

"The owner gave her double cod and chips twice and when she'd gone, rang 999."

"So why didn't they catch her?"

"Well, when our mob got there, they didn't like the look of the owner. He'd had a nasty shock, remember — " The sergeant caught sight of the inspector's face and said hurriedly:

"They thought they should call an ambulance. What they forgot was the go-slow today on behalf of the nurses. It took a while before the ambulance got there." The big man was sulky now.

"Look, if we could set up road blocks, I'm sure we'd get her — "

"Listen to me!" The inspector was standing so close his words bounced off the big thick chest. "We're not talking about a maniac — she's a little imitation terrorist, never been out of Ireland before! I know she's got a weapon but use your brain — or what passes for one — what have that cell ever done? They're dreamers, not doers! I bet five pounds that gun isn't even loaded — and I need to know what she knows! Can't you get it into your head, if the killer finds out she may have heard

140

him. . . ! And if you lot can't find one hungry leprachaun hiding out in the heather, I want somebody's resignation on my desk first thing."

As the sergeant walked away, a threat echoed down the corridor behind him: "They're always short of men for traffic duty in Pontefract. . ."

The inspector met Mr Pringle at the foot of the stairs to the Solar. "I was on my way to speak to Dr Willoughby," Mr Pringle said defensively.

"I'm not stopping you."

They climbed the staircase together, the inspector unaccountably irritable. At the top he banged on the door and muttered under his breath. Without waiting to be bidden he walked straight in, Mr Pringle close behind, into the middle of Miss Fawcett's resignation. It was an odd sensation, as though a cast were halfway through a play. No one acknowledged their entrance, the players carried on as though the two of them were invisible.

The room astonished Mr Pringle. Like the dining-room, it had remained untouched. The high ceiling absorbed the light but he was able to make out delicate stone tracery soaring upwards. On three sides, windows had thick leather curtains drawn across them. He could only guess at the clear view across the moors to the sea. Was this where Eleanor once sat, watching and waiting for Henry? Her successor stood, a heavy silk robe reflecting the firelight, hair flowing down her back. She held a silver hairbrush, the initials CRW ornately carved on the back. Mr Pringle appreciated what must be a nightly ritual — a beautiful woman in front of the vast open fireplace, brushing her hair. He had a disturbing thought: did Mrs Willoughby always play a part in a charade, never in life itself?

Centre stage, Miss Fawcett was far too deep in emotion to notice intruders. Stringy cords in her neck looked as though they would snap under the tension. "It's quite obvious that I am no longer appreciated here. . ." She waited a fraction too long for the denial that never came. "After all this time, I am still not accepted as one of — the Family." The other members of it remained impervious to her plea. "Very well then. I must consider my future — the lack of fulfilment in my present position." Had Jonathan written her lines, Mr Pringle wondered? He dreaded what might be coming next.

"I have never asked much from life but an opportunity has arisen for me to work with — with a creative man. He has invited me to be his bulwark. To stand between him and the slings and arrows of those who do not appreciate him. . ." Looking at her frail, skinny figure Mr Pringle knew she could never plug so big a gap, however hard she tried.

"Jonathan has asked me to share his load in life. I would be very foolish to let such an opportunity pass me by." Her voice had now reached such a shrill pitch that the next words, obviously intended to evoke fond memories, came out as a shriek. "He reminds me so much of Donald!"

She stopped. No one else spoke. In the frozen silence she went to the door. "I wish to leave here on Saturday."

Solid oak swung to behind her. The Colonel expelled his breath in a long, heartfelt sigh.

"Thank God for that. I thought we were stuck with her for life."

Mr Pringle could not restrain himself. "Who was Donald?"

"The one that got away," Dr Willoughby said sombrely.

The inspector cleared his throat. "A few questions, if I may. Won't keep you from your beds longer than I have to."

He's nervous, thought Mr Pringle.

"Have you spoken to the staff yet?" The question was barked. D.I. Keatley instinctively stood to attention, "Only briefly, sir."

"Should have been more thorough. Could have solved the matter by now."

"I beg your pardon, Colonel?"

"My batman. Sleeps in the Solarium, doesn't he? Bound to know what went on — "

"*He does what!*" The inspector's shout reverberated round the chamber. "Why did no one tell me before! Why wasn't it in the notes!" He stared at them, outraged, aching to go for a jugular.

His glare fell on Mr Pringle. "Wilfred Wilson sleeps in the Solarium. . . !"

"I didn't know," apologized Mr Pringle.

The Colonel jeered, "Ignorance was no excuse in my war."

Mr Pringle felt the sweat break out. Keatley's going to kill him, he thought, I know he is! And I'm going to have to watch!

He never knew how they got out of the room. He was aware of the inspector's grip on his arm, of the frozen tableau — the Colonel dominating the group, still sneering and, behind, Consuela and the doctor looking very frightened indeed. The two of them were halfway down the stairs before Mr Pringle realized neither he nor the inspector had asked the Willoughbys any questions.

In the kitchen the staff were sitting just as Mr Pringle had left them. This time there was a subtle change, was it relief? Were they waiting to begin their performance? Detective Inspector Keatley began his bull terrier routine, snapping at Wilfred.

"So you were in the Solarium last night but you didn't see fit to mention it," he challenged.

"Nobody asked me about it before."

It was irritating, unassailable: do not speak unless spoken to, never volunteer information.

"And I wasn't there all last night — "

"Tell me about it. Everything."

"I'm a bad sleeper, always have been. Neuralgia. The humidity sometimes helps."

"Did it help last night?"

"For a time. Then I woke and knew I wouldn't get off again. I got up and walked about — I often do that."

"Walked about the castle, you mean?"

"Yes."

"Did you see anyone?"

He hesitated. D.I. Keatley was in no mood for shilly-shallying. "I asked you a question," he shouted.

"Didn't see, no. I heard someone."

"What d'you mean by that?"

"In there. Hiding in my room." He pointed to a door beside

143

the fireplace. "I came back here to try and sleep some more."

Mr Pringle had assumed it led to a cupboard but now saw it opened on to a small cell, one wall being part of the great chimney breast which gave off a comforting warmth. He peered over the inspector's shoulder. On hooks once used for curing bacon hung neatly pressed clothes. A line of polished shoes marched across the deep stone windowshelf and along one wall was a small camp bed. Blankets were folded in a manner which brought back unhappy memories to Mr Pringle, of kit ready for inspection. There were no books, pictures or memorabilia to give a hint of personality. The cell was as colourless as Wilfred himself.

"You mean someone was hiding in here?"

"Yes. I tried the handle but it was locked from the inside."

The inspector examined the bolt and slid it to and fro, using the tips of his fingers.

"I think I heard it being pushed home as I came in the kitchen," Wilfred volunteered.

"Any idea who was hiding inside?"

There was no hesitation this time. He'd been waiting for the question: "Mr Powers."

The rest of the staff, hearing their cue, joined in a rondeau.

"It's happened before, you know — "

"People come in here, on the scrounge — "

"Looking for food."

"Happens all the time. They cheat."

"Don't know what's good for them half the time. They should stick to the diet — "

"Especially the liquid diet."

"One couple — you remember them Millie — they went to the village, they were actually seen eating chocolate cake, in the Dales teashop." This, the greatest crime of all, was met with a hushed silence. Mrs Ollerenshaw shook her head over it but the inspector refused to be diverted.

"What time did all this happen last night? When you came in here and found you couldn't open the door?"

"I'm not sure, sir. It was still dark. I settled myself in that chair there, to try and get a bit more sleep."

"You mean — you left whoever it was — hiding in your room?"

"I thought it was for the best, sir. He'd finished what he'd come for — there were dirty plates and cutlery — and a glass. He'd helped himself to the Colonel's port. I didn't want to embarrass him with it. I knew he'd leave when he thought the coast was clear."

"And when was that?"

"Not long. I found I couldn't sleep again so I started doing the laundry."

"Wilf often helps me do that," Jessie chimed in, "I was ever so grateful this morning."

"Where d'you do the laundry?"

They trooped through an archway. The laundry had once been the dairy. Large machines stood on a quarry-tiled floor. Overhead, floral towels blossomed in exotic rows along the racks. "He'd washed nearly every blessed thing by the time I got down," Jessie went on, "I'd set the alarm early to do them but we had a cuppa tea instead."

"What time was it then?"

"About six, wasn't it?" said Wilfred.

"About that, yes. I got up at quarter to."

"D'you live in then?" Mr Pringle remembered Jessie had given an address on the estate on his form.

"Some nights yes, because of the washing. I've got a room next to Miss Fawcett's."

"And you reckon whoever it was hiding in there. . ." The inspector pointed back at the cell, ". . . he — or she — nipped out while the machines were making a noise?" Jessie and Wilf nodded simultaneously.

"It's always happening here," Jessie told him, "folks coming in on the off-chance, nicking scraps. Quite posh people too sometimes, you'd be surprised — "

"But you neither saw nor heard anything that would confirm it was Mr Powers?"

"It must've been him," Millicent insisted. "None of the

145

ladies would've taken game pie and port. Not when there was plenty to choose from."

"Show me."

Back in the kitchen, Mr Pringle saw there were two fridges. The second, smaller one was dedicated to the Colonel's needs. It was full of meats and cheeses. Bottles of wine and port were stacked beneath one of the shelves near a window. Jessie pointed out how much food had been taken: Jonathan hadn't stinted himself. Mrs Ollerenshaw shook her head. "So much dead flesh," she muttered. "Combined with a liquid diet. . . no wonder he was so ill this morning." Jessie shut the fridge door firmly. "The Colonel's never come to any harm from what he eats." Mrs Ollerenshaw was unconvinced.

The inspector looked at his watch. "I wonder if Mr Powers has gone to bed yet?" Mr Pringle felt rather than heard a universal sigh of relief: they had played their parts well, their master and mistress would be pleased.

"I was listening to Mrs Arburthnot earlier," he said to the room in general, "and she mentioned she'd been nursing in Singapore. Can any of you confirm this?" It was a random question. The inspector cocked his head for the reply. "Nursing!" Millicent was contemptuous. "She wasn't that qualified. Turned up at the hospital one day waving some kind of certificate — we were short handed. Matron gave her a chance but she married the first patient she emptied a bedpan for."

"You were also employed at that hospital?"

"Staff nurse. I left to get married too — waste of time that was — but at least mine didn't hang himself. When we divorced madam wrote to me, offering me the job here — and paid for my training as a masseuse." The big woman was oppressive with her hero-worship. "Now that's what I call friendship. Never wanted to be paid back did she, Jessie? She's a lovely person —"

"It's typical of her too," Jessie joined in, "she's as good as she's beautiful."

"She is!" Seeing them, hot-eyed with love for Mrs Willoughby, Mr Pringle recalled an old film — *Mädchen in Uniform*, full of the same gawky schoolgirl behaviour, but those were

146

adolescents, these were grown women; it was far more disturbing.

"Was Mrs Willoughby also a nurse at that same hospital?"

They looked at him in surprise. "Madam? Whatever makes you think that? She's a lady. Came straight from finishing school to Singapore, that's right isn't it Wilf? Met the Colonel and they married soon after."

Wilfred had withdrawn into his shell. "I believe so. I met madam when the Colonel introduced her in the Mess."

That's more than you admitted before, thought Mr Pringle. But how had Millicent met her? He had a question half-framed but was too late. The inspector was gathering up his papers. The staff saw the interview was over and began putting the kitchen to rights. Mrs Ollerenshaw tended the Aga, Millicent checked the treatment chart. "Haven't I got an aromatherapy tomorrow?"

"Mrs Rees . . ." Jessie ran her finger across the paper, "at half-past eight."

"What on earth's that?"

"A massage with herbal oils. Very soothing, especially. . ." Millicent added, looking pointedly at the pair of them, "if a lady's been under stress."

As they went outside the inspector yawned. "Nearly midnight. Better see if Powers is still awake though — yes, what is it?" Wilfred had followed them. "What time tomorrow, sir? For my visit to my mother?"

"Oh, say nine-thirty. Gives me a chance to sort out a car and a driver."

"Thank you, sir. Goodnight."

They set off for the first floor. "Probably find he's scoffing another midnight feast in his dorm." D.I. Keatley was sarcastic. Mr Pringle walked quietly beside him. He was unsure of his status but he wanted very much to hear what Jonathan had to say. There was no sign of the sergeant. "Are your staff working through the night?" he asked cautiously.

"Good grief, not with the overtime rates the way they are nowadays. No, we only work golden time when it's a nice juicy rape or when a kiddie's been involved. Joe Public doesn't mind forking out extra for that."

"What if the victim is an old-age pensioner?" Mr Pringle recollected which category he came into.

"Knock off at four o'clock for tea and a biscuit." The inspector was more sad than scornful. "No publicity value in pensioners, is there?"

Inside room five all was not well. Far from being asleep, Jonathan P. Powers was engulfed by elemental forces. Passion swept Virginia Fawcett on a tempestuous wave; she rode the surf wildly. Jonathan, in danger of drowning, could not rise to the occasion.

"I love you," she shrieked, tearing his shirt, "I want you!"

The knock at the door was the most welcome sound he'd ever heard. "Come!" he cried, not summoning up hidden reserves but going down for the third time. "Come in for Chrissake! Not now, Virginia, there's someone at the door — Ah, Inspector! Do come in."

He darted about like a hostess, plumping up cushions. Seeing Miss Fawcett's disarray, the Inspector hesitated, "I trust we do not intrude?"

She looked at him with hatred, "Can't it wait?"

"Now, Virginia, we must do all we can to help the police with their enquiries." He spun her round so that she was facing him and grimaced. "Why not go and rest. . . ?" She didn't take the hint. "Pull your skirt down," he whispered, then more loudly, "We can discuss our future in the morning. Sleep . . ." he crooned, urging her towards the door, "beneficial sleep, it's what we both need after this terrible wonderful day."

She sat down firmly on a hard chair. "I'm not tired. I shall stay until you've answered their questions." Seeing him about to interrupt, she added, "I'm not leaving." There was a steeliness in her tone which all of them recognized.

"Shall we do as the lady suggests, Mr Powers?"

Jonathan glowered. He didn't want Virginia Fawcett to know what he'd been up to. He tried to brazen it out. "Well?"

"Just a few questions about last night, sir."

"I was in my room the entire time — "

"We've one witness saw you leaving it, two more people know where you were hiding when you nicked that pie, another saw you vomiting it up so, unless you tell me the truth — now — we can go to the police station and you can sit in a cell all night until your memory improves. They haven't got a very nice place here, not like we have in Salford. Two, three men banged up. Tramps, blokes who haven't had a bath in years, know what I mean — "

"All right, all right. What d'you want to know?"

"Start when you left your room. What time was that?"

"I don't know, I didn't look at my watch. I was starving, that's all I can tell you." Jonathan was sulky now.

"What happened?"

"As I say, I was desperate for food. I went to the dining-room first. There wasn't a scrap anywhere. You know, I'm beginning to doubt the wisdom of the regime here — too debilitating."

This was for Miss Fawcett's benefit but the inspector wasn't interested. "Did you see anyone?"

"No. I went to the kitchen and found a fridge stacked with the real stuff. Normally of course, I wouldn't dream — "

"Mr Powers, stick to the point."

"Yes, well . . . I had a decent meal. Washed it down with a glass or two of port — " Miss Fawcett gasped. "Oh, come off it Virginia — the prices they charge here, alcohol should be served free with every meal!"

"Mr Powers, how long were you in the kitchen?"

"I've no idea. Quite a long time. It was dark, middle of the night. I didn't rush, bad for the digestion. I was just about to leave when I heard someone coming, so I hid. There's a little room beside the fireplace — "

"That's Wilfred's," said Miss Fawcett, surprised.

"Quiet, please!" The inspector swung round, "Go on."

"I didn't want to be found out. Ridiculous really. It's the effect this place has on one. I bolted the door. Good thing I did because whoever it was tried the handle. Then started poking about with that stove — "

"Are you sure?"

"Sounded like it. Those doors make quite a clunk when you shut them. I decided to wait. I'd taken the bottle in with me so I wasn't worried. Eventually I heard a washing machine start up — maybe that's what whoever it was was doing with the boiler — heating up the water? Anyway, I decided it was time to be off. On the way back I thought I saw someone in the long corridor — someone tall, it could have been la Arburthnot, or Millicent perhaps, I'm not sure. You know, it's frightening the way people wander about this place at night."

"I'm beginning to think Dr Godfrey was the only person to spend it in bed," agreed the inspector wearily, "then what did you do?"

"Went back to my own room of course. About an hour or so later, Jessie arrived with the tea. At eight I was in Reception waiting for Miss Brown — she was late. So you see — " Virtue triumphed over petty thieving, "I'm in the clear for the entire night."

The inspector was tired. "We'll leave it at that for this evening. I shall want a new statement from you tomorrow, Mr Powers. I take it you'd rather we destroyed the first one you made?"

Jonathan should have been grateful but it wasn't in his nature. "Seeing that the policeman who interrogated me this morning was nothing better than a criminal — "

It was a mistake to try and score off Detective Inspector Keatley. "Escort Miss Fawcett back to her room, would you Mr Powers. Make him go inside and examine it thoroughly, Miss Fawcett. In fact, why not try and persuade Mr Powers to sleep on a chair, for your mutual protection? We can't be too careful at present, can we?"

Mr Pringle daren't look at Jonathan's face. He followed the inspector outside. They stood for a moment, contemplating Von Tenke's door, still locked and sealed.

"The post mortem had to be a bit loose about the time of death," the inspector told him quietly, "because they keep that swimming pool so ruddy hot. Forensic's going to do more tests tomorrow but for now. . . any time between midnight and six a.m." He shrugged expressively.

"Dr Godfrey was kind enough to give me his opinion during our chat. He indicated the contents of the stomach would have to be analysed. . ."

"One of the results we're still waiting for. Yes. . . keep forgetting it was our medical friend as well as Mr Powers who found him. Let's walk it, shall we?" They set off to retrace Valter's final journey.

They walked in silence most of the time. Once the inspector said, "It's a long way . . . a bloody long way." As they reached the ground floor Mr Pringle commented, "What a great pity . . . with so much activity going on last night, no one looked at a watch?"

"They only do that in books," said the inspector morosely. They were staring along the corridor to the entrance to the Solarium. "How long did it take to render Mr Von Tenke unconscious?"

"According to the p.m., approximately thirty seconds. Doctor thought whoever it was knew what they were doing. Deep, deep marks. No other sign of injury."

"Even so, thirty seconds is a very long time to keep up that amount of pressure."

The inspector looked at him speculatively. "What you're saying is there had to be two people."

"When he was rendered unconscious, it seems likely. Was the belt fastened then?"

"We don't know. Before death, certainly, but that only means before he was dropped into the pool. Actual death was by drowning. Come on. . ." They set off once more. "It's a hell of a way with a body," the inspector said again, then added, "He had to be conscious before they put that on him because of the buckle." Mr Pringle looked blank. The inspector explained. As he did so, Mr Pringle realized two things. One was that he had been reinstated in the inspector's confidence.

"Where is the suit of armour used to supply those particular items?" he asked.

"Not up here. These . . ." The inspector waved at 200 years of Willoughby history, "are all quite recent apparently. The medieval armour's kept downstairs near the gymnasium because of the insurance. The killer used a helmet and sword from one of those."

"How very odd," said G. D. H. Pringle.

As they walked into the Solarium, Mr Pringle stopped in astonishment. "Goodness, look at those stars!" he said. Inside the lights were dim. Suspended above, clearly visible through the geodetic panes, were sparkling jewels made more vivid by the impenetrable blackness beyond. D.I. Keatley regarded him with suspicion. "Not turning poetic on me, are you?"

"Oh no. I can never remember quotations, nor do I read or write poetry."

"That's all right then. Hate people who quote. Just reminds me of the 'O' levels I didn't get. Only the thought of the overtime keeps me going, this time of night."

Relief flooded through Mr Pringle. Perhaps there was a place for him in the scheme of things after all.

"Now then. . ." The inspector led the way to a Grecian bench, took off his coat, loosened his tie and tried to sit comfortably. "That's the second time I've retraced the route and it doesn't get any shorter. Let's go through it systematically, leave out anyone who couldn't possibly have done it and concentrate on the others. Last night everyone, including Von Tenke, is in the dining-room for dinner when Dr Godfrey and Mr Powers have their little ding-dong. Miss Pritchett rushes out followed a few minutes later by Dr Godfrey. What happens next?"

"According to more than one account, Mr Von Tenke left the room shortly afterwards, as did one or two of the other guests. No one claims to have seen him after that — "

"Apart from Mrs Arburthnot."

"Apart from her, certainly."

"Let's keep it in sequence. After the punch up, Miss Fawcett, Mrs Ollerenshaw and Mrs Burg helped patch up Powers. Guests drifted off to the library or their rooms. The staff cleared away. According to the sergeant and Robinson, the staff were all together until they left the kitchen then the girl Beverley and Mrs Ollerenshaw went home, the others went to the staff wing. Mrs Willoughby had one of her massages in the Solarium with Wilfred, the Colonel went to his study in the tower. Mrs Willoughby said the Solarium was empty when she got there — the doctor and Miss Pritchett were in room two by then. After the massage, Wilfred stayed, the rest we know about. According to Robinson's notes again, Mrs Burg locked up about eleven p.m."

"As Mrs Arburthnot is our lynchpin at this point, do we know her movements?"

"Miss Fawcett told Robinson she was the last guest to leave the library. Miss Fawcett always stays until everyone's gone, puts the fireguard in position — it was there this morning. She says she thinks she left about eleven-thirty last night. Does that tally with everything you've been told?"

Mr Pringle agreed that it did.

"Now we get to the interesting bit. Mrs Arburthnot goes to her assignation. We presume Von Tenke was alive when she left?"

"I think we must in view of Miss Kelly's reported remark. I also believe Miss Brown pushed her note under Mr Von Tenke's door after Mrs Arburthnot had left the room." Mr Pringle explained his theory. D.I. Keatley nodded.

"So the missing note is now in position. Miss Brown goes. What happens next?"

"About the same time, according to Mrs Arburthnot, Mr Powers leaves his room."

"And goes via the dining-room to the kitchen, wasn't in any rush. Finds what he wants, has a leisurely meal, hides with a bottle of port. How long does it take to do washing?"

"I allow at least an hour at the laundrette, especially if I'm using the drier," Mr Pringle answered earnestly.

"So that whole business — the meal, hiding, hearing the machine, etc. That all sounds feasible?"

"I think so."

153

"Tell me again about that business with Von Tenke when Powers nearly fell out of the window? Accused him of trying to murder him, didn't he?"

"According to Dr Godfrey, Mr Powers exaggerated."

"All the same, it happened. But did it warrant strangling a man in retaliation?"

"And has Mr Powers the temperament for such an act?"

"God knows. I don't. Must check with Wilfred about that stove. If he wasn't riddling the ashes, what was he doing — now, do we assume Miss Brown went straight back to her room?"

"I find it difficult to imagine her seducing Mr Von Tenke."

"Very true. So, we've got Mrs Rees — I'm leaving her out of the calculations for obvious reasons — in room one, the doc and Miss P. are still in two, Arburthnot's in three, Brown in four — five is now empty — A. N. Other is in six with Von Tenke and Miss Kelly hears the ruckus from number seven. She then moves to number eight and eventually the good doctor joins her — without having seen anything?"

"I think we must assume the murderer had moved the body downstairs by then. Also Dr Godfrey admitted he was tired. It's dark in that corridor. Anyone could hide behind the armour or furniture."

"True. So where's everyone else?"

The inspector eased his buttocks and listed the staff on his fingers. "Again according to Robinson's notes, Miss Fawcett, Jessie and Millicent are in their rooms — the staff wing is beyond the tower — and Miss Fawcett claims she's a light sleeper. Lies awake reading then takes Valium. Claims she didn't take any last night though and in consequence slept 'fitfully'."

"She'd had a most exciting day," suggested Mr Pringle, "far more exciting, probably, than any of her books."

D.I. Keatley grinned. "Wonder how the great Jonathan P. Powers made out tonight? Serve him right. I've had to watch enough of his programmes, because of the wife. Right, so who's left?"

"The Willoughbys," answered Mr Pringle, "but the Colonel made a particular point of stopping me in the corridor to tell me he wasn't the murderer. He said Valter was a man for whom he had a particular affection, he was most distressed by what had happened. Unfortunately I haven't had the opportunity of conversing with either Mrs Willoughby or the Colonel on the subject — "

"Neither have I, dammit." The inspector walked to the edge of the pool and kicked it moodily. "But I'm not going on any more wild goose chases. Tomorrow morning I'm interviewing the pair of them. No doubt they'll tell me they were tucked up in some antique four-poster all night."

"Their rooms are a considerable distance from Mr Von Tenke's," said Mr Pringle thoughtfully. "If they had been considering a murder, surely they could have arranged a closer proximity? Also, would one invite a person into one's castle in order to kill him?"

"Dunno. In a terraced two up two down in Salford, you invite a bloke down to the local then smash his face in, but you're right. This is Yorkshire."

The inspector stared pugnaciously at flattened greenery at the shallow end. "One of them did it. One of those we've eliminated — maybe two — lugged that big man down here, trussed him up to stop him saving himself and shoved him in over there. I'm more and more convinced there must've been two . . ." He looked at Mr Pringle who didn't argue. "So which two was it? We've gone wrong somewhere. Is there anything else you can think of? Anything you haven't told me?"

Mr Pringle looked distressed, took off his spectacles and rubbed the sore spots on the side of his nose. "I'm at a loss, I'm afraid. I think, although I have no proof, that the Singapore connection is relevant, also the fact that Mr Von Tenke may have been a blackmailer. More than that I cannot deduce at present. I must confess to being a little weary. If I might go through my own notes again carefully, I may find something we've overlooked."

Detective Inspector Keatley peered at him in the dim light.

"You're bushed. So'm I. Come on. Let's sleep on it, do us both good. Give the unconscious a chance to come up with something."

"Oh, I do not intend to sleep, Detective Inspector. I prefer to work. Order and method are most soothing. . ."

"Suit yourself." The inspector yawned so wide this time, Mr Pringle saw down the cavern of his throat. "See you in the morning."

"There is one small matter . . ."

"Yes?"

"A forename. I'll write down the details, if I may." Mr Pringle scribbled on a piece of paper. The inspector read it. "You're thinking along those lines, are you? Well, we should be able to find out."

"One of your lady policewomen. She was describing the computer, she seemed to be very knowledgeable."

"Sure. Ask her yourself. Tell her I authorized it."

"Thank you very much indeed."

The inspector climbed the Solarium steps and opened the door. He stopped. Mr Pringle waited. "Did the good doctor ever say what woke him? When he was in room two with Miss Pritchett?"

"I'm not sure. I'll need to check."

"Do that. I'd be interested to know. Goodnight to you."

"Good night, Detective Inspector."

Mr Pringle arranged his forms and notes in two neat piles and unscrewed his pen. The window was open a fraction, he had wrapped an eiderdown round his knees. He wanted to stay alert. There was only 24 hours left before he lost his chance of the drawing.

Any violent end had, he was convinced, a beginning as small as the grain of sand in an oyster but this irritation didn't grow into a pearl. It festered until all the factors came together to cause it to erupt in that moment of passion which led to death. Most of those factors he had in front of him: all he had to do was to retrace through them the event that was the beginning.

He considered again the information he had gathered. Nothing differed in essentials from the inspector's outline of events. He then began a list which, to an outsider, might have appeared a Table of Kindred and Affinity but was a careful interlocking of those relationships which he believed existed within the castle. He had not received any forms from the Willoughbys. Could he persuade Dr Willoughby to put pressure on his brother and sister-in-law? What would be a tactful approach? He considered the problem.

The room was absolutely silent. Sounds from the park and moor did not reach as far as this. Nothing distracted him until in the stillness, something moved. It was on the periphery of his vision. G. D. H. Pringle froze. In one split second all the good things in life flashed before his inner eye. He remembered it was only greed that had brought him here and made the astonishing discovery he no longer cared about Art. He simply wanted to go on living — Oh, how he wanted to live! The door was pushed further open. "I thought you ought to know something."

His tongue cleaved to the roof of his mouth. He knew if he tried to stand, his jellied knees would not support him. Instead he made a feeble gesture and Miss Brown interpreted this as an invitation to enter. She sat, facing him, her woolly dressing gown tied round the middle with a cord that separated her into two solid bundles of flesh. Her grey hair stuck up wildly. "Someone brought my note back. I found it on my dressing table. I've no idea who put it there."

Mr Pringle wondered if he could rely on his larynx yet. He cleared his throat. "Have you brought it with you?"

"No. I threw it on the fire."

"What!"

Evidence was sacred to Mr Pringle. To destroy it was wicked. "It was mine," Miss Brown protested, "I wouldn't have let anyone else but Valter read it, and he's dead."

"But it would have been proof, Miss Brown, for the police."

"No, it jolly well wouldn't! I wouldn't have let them see it!" She was flushed. "It was none of their business."

"It would at least have established your — er, position. . ."

Now he'd really upset her. "You don't believe I was telling the truth, do you?"

"My dear Miss Brown, it is not I — "

"Well I've never told fibs and I didn't tell you one this morning. I did write that note. I pushed it under Valter's door and Sheila Arburthnot was there."

"Yes, we know that."

"Oh."

He'd deflated her temporarily but she rallied. "Did you ask her about it?"

"Mrs Arburthnot made a statement to the police," he replied carefully.

"Bet she told a few fibs."

"I think — not . . ." Not in the end, anyway.

"She always used to."

He tried to appear sympathetic. "Indeed . . . ?"

Miss Brown fiddled with her dressing gown cord. "She did something unforgivable once. I knew Eric first, you see. . ."

"Ah."

Miss Brown was brick red now. "I was a bit older than he was but that didn't matter. We used to play tennis together. Mixed doubles. I was really keen, I'd had a lot of practice, you see. Eric wasn't bad and he was getting better — then she turned up. Pretended to be all sympathetic when he went into hospital for a wisdom tooth. He never played tennis after that . . ." She was near tears. Mr Pringle felt helpless.

"I'm so sorry," he said. Tears rolled down her cheeks.

"There was never anyone else . . . She was younger, she could've found another man . . . He could've got a divorce and married me. . ."

Mr Pringle stared at his desk, unseeing. One of the oldest saddest emotions, manifesting itself in raw misery, but there was nothing he could do to alleviate it. He sat and waited. Eventually there was a fierce sniff. As usual Miss Brown hadn't a handkerchief. "I'm all right now. Will you see me back to my room? The murderer might still be about."

Mr Pringle wasn't brave but neither was he unchivalrous. He

158

stumbled to his feet. "Of course," he replied.

They went out into the corridor. Mr Pringle recalled the inspector's easy assurances to the guests that men would be on duty. He couldn't see anyone. He was aggrieved. Even if overtime rates were prohibitive surely the public purse could have been stretched a little? Old age pensioners deserved some protection. Miss Brown unlocked her door. "Goodnight," she said, "do be careful on the way back, won't you."

While everyone slept, one person remained at his post, determined to prove his worth. He tip-toed into the inspector's room so as not to disturb him. In the narrow bed, a winceyette pyjama jacket was rucked up round the inspector's ears. The sergeant looked at it in disgust.

Robbie wouldn't have worn pyjamas — he wouldn't have gone to bed! Robbie was on the ball. Always worked round the clock on a murder, expected everyone else to do the same. The instant he was assigned to a case he called in the media to give them his initial impressions. After that there were twice-daily news conferences and, as soon as ITN had a unit in position, a re-enactment of the crime. This was the high spot for the sergeant. Robbie always appointed one of his team as liaison officer. Last time it had been the sergeant's turn. His breast swelled as he remembered how he had actually appeared on television, walking into shot and handing Robbie a telex. They had done five takes before the director was satisfied. The sergeant's wife had recorded the final result and the sergeant replayed the tape on their wedding anniversary.

When it had first been transmitted, his wife had insisted he buy a hairpiece. It still hung in the wardrobe and frightened him occasionally when he reached for a shirt and forgot it was there. He was equipped, eager to play his part, when this swine had put a 24-hour embargo on all press coverage.

The sergeant smiled smugly to himself. Something had happened that couldn't be embargoed. He couldn't wait to break the news. Bending low he whispered in the unconscious ear, "We've got the man, sir."

D.I. Keatley managed to control the beating of his heart long

159

enough to ask "What — man?"

"Maeve Kelly's contact. The pilot of the helicopter she was hoping to escape in." The sergeant waited until the inspector struggled upright. He was going to impress the bastard this time.

"Maeve Kelly phoned Killemorragh, reversing the charges, but the pilot, Sean O'Riley, gave the game away. He alerted the Western Defence system. They were looking west, as usual, when he flew in low from Ireland, failed to identify himself and crossed a NATO air exercise area. It was the Swiss, the first time they've ever taken part, he scared the shit out of them, poor devils. Fighter Control ordered a couple of RAF Tornados up to intercept. When O'Riley saw them he transmitted on one two one five to ask what the fuck they were playing at. They didn't manage to force him down, he ran out of fuel instead and crashed on to the M18 just south of junction four. The driver of the tanker coming in the other direction was over the legal limit. He's in Doncaster Infirmary. If he lives, we'll book him in the morning."

The sergeant needn't have worried. Detective Inspector Keatley was very impressed. "My, my . . . Fancy her finding a phone box that still works in Yorkshire. Where is it, as a matter of interest?"

"Outside Pickering police station."

"Ah. . ."

"We've got the pilot downstairs."

The inspector blinked. "Pardon?"

The sergeant realized he'd have to go more slowly. "RAF Police wanted to hand him over to Special Branch but I insisted we have a crack at him first."

"Whatever for?"

The sergeant was baffled. He could see the question was genuine. "To trap the girl, sir. We'll use Sean O'Riley as bait to force her out into the open."

The inspector sank back on his pillows. To the sergeant's horror it looked as if he was going to weep. When he spoke it was in such a low mumble the sergeant had to lean over to catch the words: "Piss off. . ."

Chapter Six

CLARISSA OPENED THE door and saw who it was. "Good morning." The phrase was polite but the tone glacial. Hugh swallowed.

"There's nothing I can do except apologize, most abjectly. I'm very, very sorry for what happened last night." He looked hungover and extremely penitent. The ice unfroze a little.

"It was so stupid — "

"Yes, I know."

"In front of Jonathan, too. He positively gloated."

"Don't Clarissa, please!"

"He and Mr Pringle had to put you to bed. I think Wilfred helped."

"Oh, no!"

"I needed you last night! I wanted someone to lean on, not another drunk — I was so frightened — I couldn't sleep for ages."

"I woke up at four. I've been sick several times, I feel like death and I love you."

"Oh, Hugh . . ."

They stood looking at each other, longing to touch, but neither moved. The door of the next room opened. "I'm ready to go down if you are," said Mrs Rees.

"Yes, of course," Clarissa turned back to him. "We're both due downstairs for treatments. Will I see you in the gym at ten?"

"Oh yes!" He didn't know how he'd cope but he'd be there.

"Yes, what is it?" Wilfred had appeared beside them.

"Excuse me sir, would you be able to have your massage earlier this morning?"

"No, I wouldn't," Hugh replied abruptly. He wasn't going to

161

be pushed around by Jonathan again, whatever the excuse.

"It's to enable me to visit my mother in hospital, sir. The police have arranged a car to take me at nine-thirty."

His stars were obviously unfavourable this morning but at least he would see Clarissa again at ten. She was walking slowly down the corridor with Mrs Rees. In the distance, Mr Pringle was talking to a W.P.C. "When d'you want me?" Hugh asked Wilfred.

"In about ten minutes, if that's convenient. I'm very grateful, sir."

The W.P.C. considered the piece of paper. "Shouldn't be a problem especially if a driving licence has ever been issued. D'you know if one has?" Mr Pringle thought quickly. "I cannot be certain but I think it likely."

"I'll get on to it straight away."

"Thank you very much."

"That's okay. Nice to have something to do." She beamed at him and Mr Pringle felt much younger.

Back in his room, the telephone rang impatiently.

"Pringle, I'm in a bit of a spot."

"Good morning, inspector. Is there any way I can help?"

"If you would. There's an unemployment march this morning — I'd completely forgotten about it — but I've had to release some men to help cover it. Point is, that leaves me a bit short. Could you accompany Wilson to the hospital? Unofficially of course, just to keep an eye. He can't stay with his mother long because he's due back here to give the men a sauna at eleven — you'd be away an hour at the most."

"But . . ." This morning the inspector was interviewing the Colonel and Mrs Willoughby. Mr Pringle dearly wanted to be there. Even if they had refused to fill in his forms, they could hardly refuse to answer the inspector's questions. And for Mr Pringle, the pieces of the jigsaw already had a pattern. He only needed to know a little more. The inspector guessed the reason for his hesitation. "Let you know if anything crops up," he said easily, "and it would be a great help to me."

162

How could Mr Pringle refuse? "Yes, of course," he said. "Good man. Half-past nine in Reception."

In the small room Edith Rees lay on a couch and stared at the ceiling. Delicate folds of pink and grey fell in soft fanlike pleats, drapery covered the walls; she was inside a sybaritic silk womb. Behind her head a gilt-framed mirror reflected a dressing table laden with glass-stoppered bottles. Millicent emerged from behind a curtain.

"I'm going to put a bit of extra support under that hip of yours. It's giving you some discomfort, isn't it?" Nursing instincts to the fore, she pushed the pillow under the gaunt body. Mrs Rees sighed with relief. A trolley laden with sweet-smelling oils was wheeled past her to the foot of the couch.

"Close your eyes and relax, madam. I'm going to take away all that tension. I can feel it under your skin — tied up in knots we are this morning." Millicent leaned across to the wall and pressed switches. The lights faded to a soft pink glow. Music came from hidden speakers. Edith Rees gave herself up to the sensual delights of bergamot and roses.

Normally she disliked piped music but this was Vivaldi. As Millicent massaged her into soft pliant ease, her mind soared free on the melody. The strong hands kneaded her scalp. Skin slipped to and fro over her skull; her eyelids were heavy with oil of lavender, the last worries ebbed away.

"I'm going to leave you to rest now and let the herbs do their work. I'll come back in about ten minutes and take you back to your room."

"Thank you."

The door shut quietly. Mrs Rees listened as Autumn drifted into Winter. She was drowsy, half asleep, when she felt her pillow being moved. "Can't I stay a little longer?" The music still played: surely ten minutes wasn't up yet? She opened her eyes and looked up to an inverted face that was completely familiar. "Oh, it's you. I'm glad you realized what I was trying to tell you last night. It's in my bag. Take it. I don't know why I didn't throw it on to the fire but I guessed you wouldn't rest till

163

you'd got your hands on it." Mrs Rees watched as her handbag was opened and the object withdrawn.

"Filthy . . ." she whispered.

"Where did you find it?" The voice was flat, almost indifferent.

"In the corridor. I'd gone to find some tea. When I found that, saw what it was, I went back to my room. I didn't see — anything."

"Close your eyes — please!"

That last word told her everything. Muscles and sinews tightened as she made a valiant effort to save herself. "But you've got what you wanted," she cried, "and I've told no one — "

"You know too much!"

Her senses blackened into unconsciousness. As she spiralled down into eternity, Edith Rees had a last terrifying thought. "I'm covered in oil — I shall burn like a torch!" But it was too late: she could no longer scream.

"Mr Pringle, Mr Pringle!" He was hurrying because he was late but he stopped, obedient to the call. It was the W.P.C. "That didn't take long, did it?" She stood in front of him, very pleased with herself.

"The name? You mean — you've discovered it already?"

"Could take some people weeks. I've got a friend in Swansea who was trained at IBM." Mr Pringle looked dutifully impressed.

"What name are you expecting?" She was young enough to want to play games, she was also very pretty. Mr Pringle said indulgently, "Shall I guess? I think it's Millicent?"

"Oh." Her face fell. "Sorry." She held out the piece of paper. Underneath his query she'd printed in rounded letters the word RITA.

"But — "

"We double checked. I told my friend this was a murder enquiry."

"I'm afraid I don't quite understand — oh dear, is that the

164

time? I must rush. Thank you. . . thank you very much for all your help." Still puzzled, he hurried away. She stood watching him go.

Wilfred and Mr Pringle arrived in Reception simultaneously. Neither spoke. Mr Pringle because he was confused: he had spent most of the night carefully piecing together his jigsaw. Now the key to it was wrong. As he got into the police car he looked at his companion. In mufti, no longer wearing immaculate white, was there ever a more colourless man? Mr Pringle plunged into deep waters.

"Your sister, the one who was sent for adoption, do you ever see her?"

Wilfred stared at him. "Why d'you ask?"

"I just wondered."

There was no reply. Wilfred turned his head away and looked out of the window, ignoring him completely. After a couple of miles the car swung left through Victorian brick gateposts.

"Was her name — Rita?"

The dark eyes were blank without a scrap of emotion. "Yes," Wilfred conceded eventually.

The Geriatric wing, formerly the Poor Law Institution, had been garishly modernized. Bright chintz, totally alien to the green and cream tiles, hung on rails dividing the beds by a regulation two feet on either side. In these cubicles, old ladies sat, each in her private world like animals in a menagerie, guarding their own spaces. Here and there an independent spirit cried out occasionally, reasserting its existence. Amid the tightly packed detritus, the West Indian Sister's smile beamed like a searchlight and generated warmth. "Hallo — you come to visit your Ma? That's good. She wouldn't sleep last night because you ain't been to see her. Hey, look who's come to see you. Look treasure, see — you got a visitor. That's better, ain't it. Now how about a bit of a smile? And another fella. That's more your style, mmm? Two gentlemen?"

She bustled them down the ward, talking constantly, in

through half-drawn curtains so that they were brought up short by the bed. Mr Pringle had imagined he would see a large, helpless woman. Instead, here was a birdlike creature, dark heavy plaits framing her bony face. There wasn't a trace of grey in the hair but the skin had a thousand wrinkles. She gazed longingly at her son but he stood silent in front of strangers.

Mr Pringle realized. "Wait outside if I may," he said awkwardly and edged back between the two rows of cubicles. "Is there anywhere?" he asked helplessly.

"Sure. In my office. Have a cup of tea." The Sister bounced her way cheerfully along the room, shouting greetings, eliciting here and there the flicker of a response. Mr Pringle was utterly cowed by it all.

Her office had a window overlooking the ward. A probationer brought in four cups of tea. "Sugar?"

"I have my own, thank you." He fished for his small plastic tube. The Sister ladled out three generous spoonsful, "Got to keep my strength up, looking after that lot. Got me on the run all day, some of them."

"Yes, indeed. Er, how many . . . ?"

"Forty-five. There was forty-six but one of them passed away last night. Listen — "

The probationer paused in the doorway.

"I'll want a strong pot ready when the next of kin arrive, okay? And tell them to leave the body in the chapel till they seen it." The girl nodded.

"Those cups," Mr Pringle asked her, "are they for Mr Wilson and his mother?"

"Yes."

"If they pass any message to each other, could you tell me what is said? It's a police matter," he explained to the Sister apologetically, "and I am supposed to keep an unofficial eye."

"That's all right. Do what he asks. Come back here and tell us after." The girl disappeared. Sister cupped both hands round her tea, "So . . . what's been going on at Aquitaine? Someone been killed, we heard."

Mr Pringle was shocked. Who had disobeyed the inspector's

166

order? As if reading his thoughts, she went on, "One of the gardeners there, couldn't go into work yesterday 'cause there's a policeman at the gate sending everyone away. He came here instead to visit his aunty — Mrs Gillie, with the blue hair-ribbon. Yoo-hoo!" She waved vigorously and in the ward, one or two hands lifted in feeble response.

"One of the guests died. . . in unfortunate circumstances," Mr Pringle said primly, "and police are investigating."

"Rich folks. . ." The Sister smiled contemptuously. "They don't need all that palaver. . . just stop eating so much." She gave him a professional scrutiny, "You don't eat cream buns, do you?"

"I have always been thin," Mr Pringle admitted.

"There you are then. Me. . . I have a doughnut at breakfast time!" She gave a rich jolly laugh. Mr Pringle tried a question.

"Why did you suggest male visitors were Mrs Wilson's preference?"

The Sister laughed again. "Did I? Well, she was chatting up the porters when she was brought in yesterday. I like it. Some of them, they don't know if it's night or day, never mind if it's got trousers on." She looked in mock despair at the apathetic rows. There was a sudden urgent wail. The probationer stopped pretending to tidy a locker. Sister banged her cup into its saucer, "Oh my God, not again!"

She hurried out into the ward, indignation pouring forth, "Why don't you ring your bloody bell? I'm sick of changin' your bed. Listen, you've been a naughty girl, haven't you? You get paper sheets till you learn not to wet yourself."

She yanked one old woman on to a commode beside her bed not cruelly but out of exasperation, pulling up her nightdress and ripping the soiled sheet off the bed. Feeling sick, Mr Pringle looked away.

"I'm ready to leave now if you are, sir?"

"So soon?"

"Mother's quite comfortable. I think she'll settle. I'll just let her know we're leaving." The Sister came back into the office. "You two off then?" She wasn't really interested, she was

167

preoccupied with counting out fresh linen. The probationer was with her. "There wasn't much said," she told Mr Pringle, "he kept telling her it was all right and she was asking when he was coming to see her again. They all ask that."

Mr Pringle walked out into the ward with her. The incontinent woman still whimpered on her commode. In the middle of the row, the one empty cubicle looked conspicuous. "At least you have one less to care for this morning."

She smiled and shook her head. An eighteen-year-old so much more worldly wise than he. "Not for long. There's a queue waiting to bring their old Mums in here, you know. We've got a good reputation."

On their drive back, there was a change in Wilfred. Mr Pringle couldn't put his finger on it. He was as silent as before but now there was an air of repose, of confidence almost. Mr Pringle was puzzled.

"They're very good to them there, did you notice, sir?"

"I beg your pardon?"

"The whole place was spotless and Mother hadn't noticed the Sister was foreign, so that's all right. I shan't have to worry about her any more, not now I know she's being well looked after." If that was all true, Mr Pringle felt sick at heart. Eventually he ventured a question. "Do you ever see anything of your sister nowadays? The one who was adopted?"

"No."

And that was all.

"I'm very worried about Mrs Rees, madam. I can't find her anywhere."

"What on earth d'you mean?" Consuela's tone was sharp.

After exercises, Detective Inspector Keatley insisted on interviewing Gerard and herself. Mrs Willoughby wasn't looking forward to it. "Have you asked Miss Pritchett?"

"Yes, madam. She's worried too. I went to help Mrs Rees back to her room but she'd disappeared. No one's seen her since."

Mrs Willoughby pulled the sash of her wrap into a tight bow.

"I'm already late. Tell Virginia. She can organize a search party. Mrs Rees can't have gone far."

"I haven't seen Miss Fawcett either this morning, madam." The beautiful nostrils flared with anger. "Then when you do, remind her from me she has one more day here before she's worked out her notice. She can begin it by finding Mrs Rees." And Consuela sailed off to the gymnasium.

But Beverley needed a clean overall. And she made the terrible discovery.

In the library, Jonathan was frantic. He'd met an immovable object. Never before had he paid such a high price for laundry. Virginia Fawcett had him in her sights and he couldn't escape.

"It's not as though you're engaged to Miss Pritchett," she insisted, "so there's no impediment. We could be married by Special Licence the day after tomorrow — "

"Oh, I'm sure it takes longer than that!" If it didn't, he'd go on his knees to the Archbishop of Canterbury, beg him to refuse. "I'm deeply touched by your suggestion, Virginia, don't misunderstand, but what I don't think you realize is that deep down you are still searching — not for a husband, dearest, nothing as mundane as that — but The Real You. It's your birthright Virginia, the most exciting search any of us can undertake. You, I know, are still asking yourself with every waking breath — 'Who am I?' Tell me I'm right."

This had worked wonderfully well some weeks previously with an over-eager make-up lady at the BBC. Miss Fawcett was of a different calibre. She came at him, rabbity teeth bared eagerly, "What nonsense, Jonathan. I know perfectly well who I am and what I want. I want to leave here and marry you."

"But Virginia, until you are truly aware of who you are, I think you should stay at Aquitaine." He was running out of ideas fast.

"Jonathan, I'm sick of knowing who I am. I've known who I was for fort. . . for thirty-eight years. Oh, go away!" For the library door had opened and a W.P.C. was ushering in Clarissa and Mrs Arburthnot, "Kindly leave," cried Miss Fawcett, "this is a private conversation!"

"Detective Inspector Keatley's orders, I'm afraid," replied the W.P.C. "Everyone is to come here and wait until further notice."

"We'd only just arrived in the gym," explained Clarissa, "when we were told to come up here. By the way, have you seen Edith, Jonathan?" He shook his head.

Mrs Arburthnot was at a loss, too. "I don't know what's going on," she said crossly, "I was looking forward to a peaceful, healthful day. At least you can tell us the reason now we are here." The W.P.C. took up her official stance and stared straight in front of her. "I'm sorry madam. I have to obey orders."

Jonathan was light-headed. "Never mind, never mind," he warbled, "it's absolutely normal. Happens every time. In the final scene the police tell everyone to go to the library then they come in and announce who the murderer is." He'd directed so many Agatha's that ended that way. They were a piece of cake provided one didn't mess about with fancy angles. One thing was certain, he'd been provided with a breathing space.

The inspector had never been so angry in his life. He shouted at Hugh, "I didn't say you could stop! Keep at it — that's an order!"

"It's no use. . ." Hugh sank back on his heels exhausted, wiping sweat from his eyes. "She was a gonner when we got here — you know it, I know it, he knows it — "

"I'm afraid he's right." Harley Street and Pinner were in accord in the final analysis, "Mrs Rees is dead, Inspector."

"I'm not going to bash her about any more either," Hugh told him.

"Powers will want to see her. Has anyone told him yet?"

"No. . ." Faced with the inevitable, the inspector hit the wall with his fist, "and you'd better see to the girl."

Tom Willoughby went white. "Dear God — you're not telling us there's been another — ?"

"The girl who found Mrs Rees. She's hysterical, suffers from asthma. We took her out to our waggon but one of you had better have a look at her."

"I'll go." Hugh was on his feet, wanting the easier task. "You can look after Powers, Willoughby." He hurried off, a constable at his heels. "He's to go to the library afterwards," the inspector called and the constable understood. No one was to be left on his own in Aquitaine this morning.

An officer entered the library and went directly to Jonathan.

"Mr Powers, would you come with me, please."

"Whatever for?"

"Detective Inspector Keatley would like to see you in his office." Miss Fawcett's eyes grew round. She screamed, "It's you! You did it! They've come to say who the murderer is, and it's you!" Quick as a flash, Jonathan seized his cue, his instinct for survival heightened by desperation, "Virginia," he said, his voice heavy with implication, "where there is no trust, how can there be love?" He left before she could think of a reply.

As Mr Pringle re-entered Reception, the area was teeming with police. He was hurt: why should he have been despatched to the hospital? All the same, it hadn't been a fruitless journey. After his brief conversation with Wilfred, he'd examined his ideas in a new light; a plausible alternative pattern was beginning to emerge. He wanted to put it to the test. Detective Inspector Keatley stood in front of him saying something.

"I beg your pardon, Inspector? My mind was elsewhere. . ."

"I said — Mrs Rees has been killed." Mr Pringle stared stupidly at him. "Stifled, we think. About an hour or so ago. She was resting after therapy. The killer dumped her body in the cupboard next door."

Mr Pringle's head was whirling. His first reaction was that Edith Rees had been spared a geriatric ward.

"You understand — she was murdered."

"But . . ." Mr Pringle scarcely knew how to explain, "Milli-cent isn't Rita." It was the inspector's turn to stare, "Where's Wilson?" he asked.

"Still outside, I think."

"You — find him and stay with him. I'll see him directly I've spoken to Colonel Willoughby." A man moved swiftly. "Whoever it was isn't getting away with it this time." Anger surged through the inspector in waves: a killing had been committed while he was on the premises — it was a personal affront. "Forensic are with the body now," he told Mr Pringle, "you can go and take a look if you want."

"No, no . . . thank you, but no." Mr Pringle stretched his hands out in front of him to prevent the idea coming closer. "However I would like to speak to Mrs Willoughby, if you have no objection."

"I thought you wanted to be there when I talk to the Colonel."

Mr Pringle was about to explain why he wanted to see Consuela first when several things happened.

Wilfred came in with his escort, then Jonathan appeared from the direction of the library.

"If you'd like to wait in my office, Mr Powers, I'll be there directly." They watched him disappear, Wilfred waiting patiently. The front door opened again with a crash. The sergeant, with traffic police on either side, rushed in with a bundle, pushing Wilfred out of their path. They deposited their offering in front of the inspector and the sergeant unveiled it with a flourish. "Maeve Kelly, sir."

D.I. Keatley sighed. He saw what he knew to be a potential witness now transformed into an incipient martyr. "I'm very sorry about all this, Miss Kelly," he apologized, "would you like a cup of coffee?"

"Sir — !" The sergeant was so full of indignation the inspector poked him in the chest to make him subside. "Now you listen to me. . . I'm still hoping Miss Kelly will agree to tell us what she knows, so you take her to the kitchen, give her coffee — bacon and egg if you can find such an article in here — but don't lay a finger on her — Got that?" The fleshy sulky mouth pouted. D.I. Keatley's eyes narrowed. "While you've been playing Starsky and Hutch, our killer's struck again, sergeant."

Mr Pringle tried to move invisibly on his way to the Solar but

Miss Brown spotted him. "Oy!" she called.

"Later, if I may." She wasn't to be denied.

"It's urgent, Mr Pringle, it's about Sheila Arburthnot." He stopped reluctantly.

"I asked her this morning — she said she didn't kill Valter. I'm sure she wasn't fibbing either."

"Yes, Miss Brown, we know that."

"Which means someone else did."

"We know that, too."

She hesitated, uncertain how to explain. "There was a bit of gossip about Valter — he wasn't popular, you know. Then the Colonel married, so that was all right. . ." Her voice trailed away because she was embarrassed but she hadn't finished. "I shouldn't have said that to you, about Sheila — but I was so worried about my note. Valter wanted money. . . he said he'd tell, about the way Daddy died. . ." Miss Brown's eyes implored, "It wasn't true, what he said — " Mr Pringle daren't be diverted further. "May we discuss that at some other time, Miss Brown?" She was offended. "I thought you'd understand. I thought you *wanted* to know." He began sliding away from her. She called after him, "Dr Willoughby was looking for you. He wondered where you'd got to."

"Later!"

Wild energy propelled him. He couldn't explain afterwards why he'd ignored the small voice inside, begging him to slow down, to reconsider the facts. He raced up the circular staircase to the room with its tracery ceiling. The leather curtains were pulled back, the view over the moors stupendous, but Mrs Willoughby wasn't there. He pressed on down a curving passage to where the rest of the Willoughbys' suite was situated. The same energy suffused him. He didn't wait to hear anyone bid him enter but pushed open a door then stumbled, blinded by light.

He was high on a bridge linking the keep with the main body of the castle, suspended in space. Windows on either side let in sunlight but it was mirrors that turned these beams to scintillating sharp lasers, mirrors that covered every square

173

inch of wall. White floors and ceiling increased the glare, adding to unreality. Mr Pringle was dazzled.

He blinked. A row of other Pringles blinked back at him, their two-day-old shirts stretching back to a grubby infinity. He recovered to find Mrs Willoughby watching him. She moved and a thousand other Consuelas glided sinuously, high priestesses in this inner sanctum of a temple dedicated to body worship.

Just as suddenly, his energy evaporated. "So sorry to intrude. . . ." Was the white and chrome object a chair? He'd risk it.

"It's about Mr Von Tenke's death. I believe that you yourself are implicated, Mrs Willoughby, possibly without ever realizing it. May I explain?" These were uncharted quicksands; he must tread carefully.

"Please do."

Had she been ugly, perhaps he would have noticed her edginess.

"It is only guesswork in part," he admitted, "but I believe the tragedy here began several years ago with the illegitimate birth of a sister to Wilfred Wilson. Mrs Willoughby, your middle name — is it Rita? And were you adopted?"

The laughter was as cruel as the silver white light. It bounced off hard surfaces, shattering his new pattern to fragments. "My baptismal names are Consuela Renata — and my family can trace its roots back to the Norman conquest — Adopted!!"

She was savage, a she-cat in her anger. He was saved by Tom Willoughby. The doctor came hurrying in, "Oh, there you are Pringle, I've been looking everywhere — Consuela, you all right?" He paused momentarily as she tried to control herself but his news was too big to wait. "Mrs Rees has been killed."

Her hysteria stopped abruptly.

"What. . . . ?"

When Mr Pringle spoke, his voice seemed to belong to someone else. It sounded to him a long way away. "I don't know why Wilson had to kill her, too, or whether indeed it was

174

he. I think it must have been. It seems unlikely that there are two murderers present in Aquitaine."

His words dropped like small pebbles into a pool. The ripples spread further and further, then the water became still again. "Wilson? Are you sure, Pringle?"

His body was weary but his brain was racing, "Oh yes, it must have been, it's the reason why I have not yet been able to fathom — oh, but of course!" There was a final shift; the last piece slid into place. He spoke without thinking, "Colonel Willoughby is a pervert, isn't he?"

It was a dreadful accusation. His ears burned as he heard himself say it but neither the wife nor the brother denied it. Mr Pringle looked at them. Tom Willoughby was stony-faced. "It's not something we boast about," he said coldly.

Detective Inspector Keatley expected many different reactions from Jonathan, he hadn't anticipated dignity. They stood looking down at the dead woman. She lay at an awkward angle, her body covered with a sheet, her face blue-grey in death. Jonathan knelt and kissed her on the cheek very, very gently. "Sorry, sweetheart," he whispered, "you shouldn't have had to go like that." He stroked her hair then got to his feet. "Can I tell Clarissa? She and mother were very close."

"Of course." The inspector was relieved at such a simple request. "Take Mr Powers upstairs. Find a room where he can have privacy — yes, what is it?" Another minion had arrived with a message.

"All right. Ask the Colonel if he wouldn't mind waiting a bit longer. Sorry, Mr Powers, I'll have to leave you."

"Do Clarissa and I have to stay on here? In Aquitaine?"

D.I. Keatley thought quickly, "I don't see why, provided you remain in the vicinity. There's a pub in the village does bed and breakfast, that suit you?"

"Yes."

"Shouldn't take long to clear up now."

"You've no idea — ?"

"We're nearly there, Mr Powers, nearly there." This was

optimism, not confidence. "The officer will take you to Miss Pritchett."

In Reception, Mrs Burg stared at a retreating back. "My, my. . . fancy her turning up. D'you think I should warn him?" she asked the W.P.C. manning the switchboard.

"No. Got the makings of a first-class 'Domestic', that has. Keep well out of it, that's my advice. I'm surprised they let her through the gate but there you are." She shrugged before adding, "I've known murder happen in a 'Domestic'." It was an unfortunate observation under the circumstances but it didn't upset Mrs Burg. She'd never known such an exciting time. "Looks like being another busy day," she said happily.

Dr Willoughby and Mr Pringle were in the Solar.

"Can you explain how it happened?" Tom Willoughby asked.

"Yes, I think so. I'm sorry your brother is implicated — "

"Gerard said he didn't do it and I still believe him," the doctor insisted stubbornly.

"No doubt he was telling the literal truth but he was undoubtedly the instigator. I'm afraid in law he will be judged equally culpable."

Tom Willoughby walked over to a window. "This could finish us, you know, the Willoughbys of Aquitaine." Mr Pringle was silent. "Go on. Explain precisely how it was done. There may be a way out for Gerard."

Mr Pringle's attitude hardened. He was beginning to realize Tom Willoughby's devotion to truth was less than his own.

"I believe it began when your brother met Valter Von Tenke unexpectedly in London. I think, though I cannot prove it, that Mr Von Tenke had some hold over the Colonel?"

The doctor said shortly, "They were lovers. Before Wilfred came along."

"Yes, I see. So there could have been a reason?"

"Possibly."

"Your brother invited Mr Von Tenke up here intending, I

believe, to dispose of him. He chose this particular week because of the various links with Singapore — Miss Brown, Mrs Arburthnot and so on — probably to try and hoodwink the police."

"He may succeed." Tom Willoughby was cheering up. "They can be fools." Mr Pringle looked at him levelly, "Your brother went too far. Had Wilson been left to do the murder on his own, we now know what *he* would have done. He would have stifled Von Tenke in the same way he killed Mrs Rees. Murderers very seldom change their ways. But those sadistic touches, that helmet and sword for instance, they were surely your brother's idea?" Tom Willoughby's smile was ghastly, "He always loved dressing up when we were children, 'the sword and cap of honour'. . . ."

Mr Pringle, who had progressed no further than cricket, continued: "Drowning a man while he was still alive and helpless was such a vicious act, I couldn't believe Wilson capable of it." His quiet voice didn't tremble as he pronounced judgement. "That, too, was undoubtedly your brother's idea."

"But there's no proof is there? You can't prove any of it?"

"No, I cannot. That is for the police. You engaged me to discover the murderer and I have done so." Mr Pringle's voice grew stronger, "Your brother was heard in Mr Von Tenke's room. I didn't understand when Dr Godfrey described to me his conversation with Miss Kelly, her words as I recall were, 'He should be ashamed. The Colonel's got it in for me because of that bloody dog'. Both Dr Godfrey and I assumed she was referring to Von Tenke. I now believe that 'He' referred to the Colonel."

"I doubt if that would stand up in court either. I mean — who's likely to believe that Irishwoman?"

"Later that night, Wilfred Wilson was heard shutting the door of the kitchen stove. He may have been destroying evidence. Afterwards he washed a great many towels — the inspector and I saw them. I think he and your brother wrapped the body in those towels to carry it down to the Solarium, they'd have to wrap it in something, and the inspector is not convinced that anyone could have managed that burden single-handed.

"There's still no proof, Pringle. Nothing tangible."

"Later that night again, Jonathan Powers saw a figure in the distance at the end of the long corridor. He thought it to be either Mrs Arburthnot, or Millicent — both tall women. I think it was your brother. Did his predilection for dressing up include female garments?"

Tom Willoughby's anger flared briefly. "My God, when I think how much Gerard's cost us over the years. Bribing parents of boys at prep school — Marlborough was a nightmare — then he insisted on going to Sandhurst. If only he'd gone in the Foreign Office as father wanted him to, none of this would have happened!"

Mr Pringle thought of England but let this pass. "Wilfred Wilson became your brother's batman in Singapore?"

"Of course. We've blessed the day Wilfred arrived. He's always been discreet. Valter never was."

Mr Pringle remembered Miss Brown's account. "Was that about the time your brother married?"

"Yes."

"What I confess I don't understand is *why* your brother married?"

"Oh, don't be so middle class, Pringle. In our family, it's expected. Besides, we had to do something about Gerard — he and Valter were getting themselves talked about. It wasn't the permissive society then, you know, never has been in the army anyway. Consuela was the perfect answer. Her family knew ours, knew the problem. We all knew she wouldn't make any demands on him because she's the same way inclined. She and Millicent suit each other very well. It's been the ideal solution."

Mr Pringle's middle class soul was reeling but he now understood why some women reacted to Consuela in the way they did and why her wondrous beauty failed to arouse him: it was directed only at female worshippers.

"I think Gerard's got a very good chance, if he keeps his head. He's been in tighter situations."

"There is also the matter of Edith Rees."

Tom Willoughby shrugged. "Why on earth did Wilson — if it was Wilson — do it?"

"Presumably because she knew something incriminating."

"Well it certainly wasn't Gerard who killed her and as she can no longer talk, we're in the clear."

Mr Pringle discovered he was furious. Perversion of the body was not his concern, perversion of the truth was.

"There is the buckle, discovered in Mr Von Tenke's dead hand. It has been sent to a laboratory for testing — "

"Keep our fingers crossed, Pringle, keep cool."

"And Mr Von Tenke has been blackmailing people. He must've been as surprised to see Miss Brown and Mrs Arburthnot as they were to see him but that didn't stop him getting up to his old tricks — "

"But is there any proof of that?"

Mr Pringle remembered Mrs Arburthnot's humiliation. Would any woman be prepared to stand up in open court and describe that ordeal? Of course not. She'd deny it ever happened.

"Miss Brown burned her note, too. Wilfred must have returned it when he took the Thermoses round but then she threw it on the fire," he answered dully.

Tom Willoughby hadn't any idea what he was talking about but realized it was good news. "There we are then. Besides, Melody Brown is fond of Consuela, she wouldn't want to do anything to hurt her." He stood, jingling coins confidently in his pocket, "With a bit of luck, I think we can avoid any unpleasantness. There's nothing *material* to implicate Gerard. We'll engage a first-class man to defend Wilson, naturally."

Mr Pringle could not bring himself to speak. For three centuries the Willoughbys had held up two fingers to the rest of the world; the arrogance of their motto, 'We Shall Overcome', stunned him with its stark reality. Tom Willoughby took his silence for tacit agreement. "Shall we go down? Gerard and the inspector have probably finished their little chat by now. By the way, Edith Rees . . . I don't think there'll be any difficulty. Old-age pensioner with a dicky heart — I examined her myself, remember. As for the other, so long as we keep the sexual side discreet, keep it out of the tabloids, we should manage."

Mr Pringle finally rebelled. "I shouldn't worry. When the public find out about the events up here, you'll be booked solid for years."

On their way to the inspector's office, Tom Willoughby's confidence grew. "Glad all this won't disappear. Pity if it had to be sold up. Bad for the Nation. You read about it every day in the papers — antiques going abroad — vandalism. Consuela's put a lot of effort into this place. We don't make a fortune, not like Longleat or Woburn, because they've kept their titles and appeal to the masses. Personally I prefer starving a few snobs to feeding lions." He was prepared to humour Pringle now he knew Gerard would escape. "When did you work all this out?"

"Last night. My mistake was to assume Wilson had done it for the sake of Mrs Willoughby. I thought she was his illegitimate sister who was sent for adoption."

Dr Willoughby stopped in his track, all geniality gone, "Good grief, Pringle, are you off your rocker? Where's your sense of decorum? There were bastards in Consuela's family, naturally, but they were fathered by Royalty — their parents were always married. You don't go round calling people like that illegitimate!"

The gulf established between the classes in 1066 loomed as wide and deep as ever. Mr Pringle bowed his head in acknowledgement of it.

Husband and wife faced each other: the physical space could be measured in metres but as between two people, it couldn't be bridged. Hugh was twisting the postcard in his hands. The message on it was crude, written, he supposed, after Valter had seen Clarissa and himself in the Solarium that night. Hugh's address had been in the register. Sending the card must have been one of Valter's last acts on earth.

"It's not true, is it?" Marion asked. "What he says?"

"Yes. Why did you come here?"

She sagged as though she'd been hit. Suddenly Hugh

realized that she'd never expected that answer. Normally he had to endure a torrent of abuse whenever they had a confrontation, a flaunting of her sexuality, this time there was nothing.

"Why, Marion?"

"I'll give up Ben, if that's what you want?"

"No. I want a divorce."

That opened the flood gates. Hate coarsened her features as it poured forth: she'd never let him go, she'd worked too hard building up the practice, she was entitled to her share of his pension, now he'd done this, if he even tried to leave, she'd make such a scandal. . ." Her voice trailed away. For the first time Marion began to realize how useless threats were. Hugh was looking at her with pity.

"I never meant it," she pleaded now, "I only taunted you, saying I wanted a divorce."

"It's far, far too late. Do you know how long it is since you and I could honestly say we loved each other? Years. Perhaps it's my fault. I tried to make a go of it, waiting all this time because I was unwilling to admit we'd failed. Maybe that drove you to make a fool of yourself with Ben, we'll never know. But whatever we did have died an awful long time ago. We both know it. I'll be as fair as I can be over money but I am going to divorce you, Marion. I hope you'll agree so that there isn't any wrangling. I've had a glimpse of paradise, I'm not letting it disappear if I can help it."

This was cruel but he'd had to endure so much in the past. She took the postcard and snapped her handbag shut on it.

"She'll grow tired of you, you'll see."

"I'm frightened already by that, never fear. But I want to spend the rest of my life making her happy if she'll let me. I've never wanted anything so much before."

She looked at him and gave her contemptuous valediction: "You weren't much of a catch. You were the best the golf club had to offer — it must've been a bad year. She'll find out."

Marion couldn't hurt him any more. Hugh wanted to cheer. Instead he said, "Thanks."

"I'll see the solicitor in the morning."

She slammed the door and he picked up the phone. He couldn't wait to tell Clarissa the glorious news.

On their way to find the inspector, Mr Pringle and Tom Willoughby were overtaken by Hugh. Mr Pringle was deeply unhappy. How not to betray his employer and yet serve the course of justice was beyond his powers. As Hugh rushed past with barely an acknowledgement, Mr Pringle forgot about his own dilemma.

"Dr Godfrey looks ill," he murmured to his companion.

"Ulcer," Tom Willoughby replied promptly. "Spotted it the moment he walked into my consulting room. He hadn't done a thing about it of course. G.P.s seldom do. They're terrified of what the diagnosis might be. I warned him but I doubt whether he'll take my advice. If he doesn't, well. . ." And Dr Willoughby shook his head over Hugh's shrinking life expectancy.

"I suppose it's always wise to have a check-up?" Mr Pringle asked nervously.

"Dear me, certainly. I sincerely hope, Pringle, you are not one of those who think 'It can never happen to me'. At your age I'd have one every six months."

The inspector welcomed them with open arms, "Come in, come in. We've got a confession."

Hugh found Clarissa in the car park. He couldn't believe it when Mrs Burg told him she was leaving but there she was, helping Jonathan load the car.

"You weren't going without even seeing me!"

She flushed. She'd been crying and her papery skin looked transparent. "Hugh, I'm sorry. . ."

"We must talk — please!"

She looked helplessly at Jonathan who shrugged, then she walked over to Hugh. "You know about Edith?"

"Yes, I'm sorry. It was too late. There was nothing Willoughby or I could do."

"I understand." She stood, fiddling with her gloves, "I can't possibly leave him now, you do see that? Not after — he can't cope on his own."

"Clarissa! You're not going back to him?"

She stared, big-eyed. "I owe it to Edith."

"Of course you don't! Oh love, we both know that isn't true. Okay he needs you now, you both need each other, to help get over the shock — but that's all, girl, and you know it."

She wouldn't look at him. "Clarissa, I love you. And I've asked Marion for a divorce."

"You've spoken — to your wife?"

"She turned up here this morning. Von Tenke sent her a postcard." He stopped.

"I don't believe it!"

"It's true, every word. He saw us that night in the Solarium — "

"Oh, no!"

"Clarissa. he's dead. None of that matters any more. I've told Marion I want a divorce because I want to marry you. She's given in — she's agreed!"

"I can't think straight. . . not yet." She gave him a painful twisted smile. "Would you have asked for a divorce if she hadn't turned up?"

"Of course I would. Oh love, don't let Edith's death make you bitter. You're the most wonderful thing that's ever happened to me — but I want you openly, honestly, as my wife. Will you wait? I promise I'll be as quick as I can." Still she didn't speak.

"As soon as I'm free, I shall go and see your father and demand your hand in marriage — "

"What?"

"Even if he lives in a place like this," Hugh gestured wildly at the castle behind him, "I shall tell him my diagnosis: you're underweight and need looking after. Prescription: take one middle-aged G.P. — "

"He lives in a flat in Kensington."

"Thank heavens for that. You can get there on the tube from Pinner — I love you so much. I want to look after you —

please. . . ?"

She managed a small grin. "Perhaps. Come and ask me again. When you're free."

He knew he couldn't expect any more from her, not yet. He peeled back one of the woollen gloves and printed a kiss on her palm. "That's on account."

There was a change in the inspector. He was jovial, Mr Pringle realized.

"Wilfred Wilson. Both killings. Gave a complete statement about half an hour ago. All nice and neat for the Coroner's Court."

Mr Pringle sensed the tension in Dr Willoughby but had to ask the question, "Did he say whether he'd managed it all — alone?"

"Oh yes. Completely solo. We took him through it thoroughly but he was unshakeable. Said he'd met Von Tenke out in Singapore and gone to parties organized by him, drug parties for pretty sailor boys and soldiers. Wilson claims he was forced to become a male whore — sorry about that, doctor. I don't suppose you or the rest of the family had any idea. Wilson wasn't expecting to see Von Tenke ever again but when he turned up here and recognized him, Von Tenke began blackmailing Wilson. He insisted Wilson came to his room, that night. . . some of the details were pretty sordid, I can tell you. Anyway, when the opportunity arose, Wilson took it and throttled him. Tried to cover up what he'd done with the helmet and by dumping the body in the pool. He swears he managed to stagger down all those stairs on his own. When I pointed out Von Tenke died by drowning, Wilson started to cry. Claims he thought the man was already dead.

"We taxed him with Mrs Rees, and Wilson said he'd destroyed the evidence against him but she found the one thing he'd dropped. Not very nice, is it. . ."

Dr Willoughby and Mr Pringle looked at the photograph; the two figures were clearly Valter and Wilfred.

"Wilson knew he'd lost this. Mrs Rees hinted she'd got it.

The rest we know about."

"Did you interview the Colonel?" asked Mr Pringle. Tom Willoughby stiffened slightly.

"Yes. . ." D.I. Keatley was expansive, "and had a word with Miss Kelly. She said it was the Colonel she'd heard in Von Tenke's room but he explained all that. Perfectly straightforward. Says he always makes a point of checking the comfort of his personal guests himself, before retiring." The inspector lowered his voice, "He told me one other thing too, in confidence. Said he hadn't been in his room the entire night. He's got — other arrangements — when Mrs Willoughby isn't feeling up to it. Thought we should know about it because someone might have seen him wandering about and said so. No need to mention that in the report, though."

Dr Willoughby was emphatic. "No need whatsoever."

"I suppose," said D.I. Keatley a trifle wistfully, "in a place like this, alternative arrangements are regarded as quite normal. In Salford, it's not the same."

Wilfred's farewell was extremely moving. The inspector watched in astonishment. "You know you've got to hand it to these aristocratic families," he said to Mr Pringle, "they really do look after their staff. If you or I had done what he did, would we be offered our place back here afterwards? Not on your Nellie. And I heard Mrs Willoughby telling him she'd visit his mother." He looked at his watch and gave a warning cough. "Time we were off, sir." The Colonel relinquished his batman's hand.

In the Partenavia Victor, Tom Willoughby shouted above the noise of the engines, "I have to admit, Gerard never said he hadn't *killed* Valter, but that he hadn't *strangled* him."

"Of course," Mr Pringle bellowed back, "and that is precisely why I told you he was equally culpable. Mr Von Tenke died by drowning."

Tom Willoughby thumped the instrument that wasn't working a couple of times, "It doesn't matter though, does it? The man's dead. Involving Gerard won't bring him back —

and Wilfred certainly killed Mrs Rees off his own bat. I'm eternally grateful to you for all your hard work. Why not leave matters as they are, now that Gerard's in the clear?"

The handbrake was on, the doctor gave the engines maximum revs and Mr Pringle filled both lungs to give a final mighty shout. "He's only in the clear until the police realize a third person must have taken that photograph."

Tom Willoughby eased the throttle, "Oh that," he said, with complete lack of concern, "don't worry about that, Pringle. We can always think of a convincing explanation for a photograph." He lined up, ready for take-off.

About a week later two people sat in room 22 at the National Gallery. Also in the room were the usual selection of tourists — French, German, Japanese plus two Americans encased in transparent plastic against nuclear fallout, searching for portraits of the royal family. Mr Pringle waited until they had moved on.

"You can see why that picture reminds me of you?"

Mavis Bignell stopped worrying about the package they'd handed in at the cloakroom and gave the 'Judgement of Paris' her full attention.

"Well," she said eventually, "none of them went to Weight Watchers did they, and I am only size sixteen, but I do see what you mean, dear. From the neck down I grant you, but she is thicker round the back. As you know, I carry all mine in front." She leaned forward to make a closer examination, "Not a single blond hair on her you know what, though, is there, and mine's as bright as the day it first grew. Who'd you say painted it?"

"Rubens."

"I prefer yours."

Mr Pringle blushed and realized that whatever its faults, English was still a universal language. "They do quite a decent cup of tea here, in the place downstairs."

A little later she said, "I shall be relieved when we've got that thing back to your place and on the wall. Where are you going to hang it?"

"Over my desk in the study."

"Yes . . . ?" She paused, the last piece of chocolate cake halfway to her lips, "Yes, I think it'll look nice there." She was still shaken by the cost, "You will remember to get it insured?"

"Yes."

"That bit of business up north must've turned out all right then?"

He sighed. "Not really. I handed a copy of my notes to the police but I fear their inference has been ignored. One culprit has escaped, scot-free."

"Tut, tut, tut. . . Never mind. The chap who hired you must've been satisfied, otherwise he wouldn't have paid up — no, I won't have another, thanks. I've got a steak and kidney in the automatic for our supper."

They finished their tea in silence. She wished he'd cheer up. "What was it then, dear, fraud? You're usually much more perky after a fraud."

"It was murder. A crime of passion although not in the accepted sense."

"Oh, well. I've always said, they do things differently in Yorkshire."